KU-635-204

THE AWAKENING HEART

When Tamsin's uncle and aunt take a holiday, leaving the family business — Lambourne Catering — in the charge of the younger generation, everyone must pitch in. Working at a near-disastrous dinner party, Tamsin meets Fraser, whose initially abrasive attitude hides a warm and understanding man beneath. Despite herself, Tamsin feels a growing attraction to him. But Rob, the man who broke her heart years ago, has returned — and seems to be carrying a torch for her once more . . .

JEAN M. LONG

THE AWAKENING HEART

Complete and Unabridged

LINFORD
Leicester

First published in Great Britain in 2015

NORFOLK LIBRARY AND
INFORMATION SERVICE

SUPPLIER	ULVE
INVOICE No.	
ORDER DATE	24·4·15
COPY No.	

First Linford Edition
published 2014

Copyright © 2015 by Jean M. Long
All rights reserved

A catalogue record for this book is available
from the British Library.

ISBN 978–1–4448–2444–5

Published by
F. A. Thorpe (Publishing)
Anstey, Leicestershire

Set by Words & Graphics Ltd.
Anstey, Leicestershire
Printed and bound in Great Britain by
T. J. International Ltd., Padstow, Cornwall

This book is printed on acid-free paper

1

'Come on, Cathy — it's time we were on the road,' Alec Lambourne told his wife.

Cathy turned to the three young people sitting round the kitchen table. 'Promise you'll ring if there's a problem,' she implored.

'Yes, of course,' her daughter Vicki assured her, 'but there won't be. We'll manage just fine — you'll see.'

Charlie stood up and slung an arm around his mother's shoulders. 'Chill out, Mum. We'll all be here when you get back, and the catering business will be thriving; won't it, Tamsin?'

Tamsin Lacey nodded. 'Absolutely. I've got all your lists to hand, Aunt Cathy, and Harvey's working like a beaver on the buffet for Lisa Clancy's wedding.'

Cathy frowned. 'I ought never to have

let Alec talk me into this holiday. The timing's all wrong. There's far too much going on here.'

'But it's nothing we can't cope with,' Vicki told her calmly.

She and Charlie followed their parents out into the hall, but Tamsin hung back, letting her cousins go first. Looking over her shoulder, Cathy stretched out a hand to her niece. 'I really appreciate you looking after the business like this, love. This trip to Norfolk means a lot to your uncle and me, but I feel as if I'm throwing you in at the deep end — expecting you to manage Lambourne Caterers while we're away. It's a big responsibility.'

'It's no problem,' Tamsin told her sincerely. 'It's not as if I've got to do any cooking with Harvey around to sort everything out, is it now?'

Cathy smiled, 'No, he's an excellent chef — but you, Tamsin, are the one that sees to the smooth running of the business.' She hugged her niece. 'I don't know what we'd do without you.'

Alec looked pointedly at his watch. 'We really do need to get a move on if we want to get there this side of Christmas.'

Vicki laughed. 'Anyone would think you were going to the other side of the world instead of Norfolk. Now, off you go. Some of us have got places of work to go to.'

Cathy gave her daughter a hug too and said quietly, 'Don't worry about that little matter that's cropped up concerning The Chocolate House. Problems have a habit of resolving themselves.'

'Hmm, well, I'm not sure this one will,' Vicki told her mother. 'Anyway, there's not much Bruce and I can do about it, is there? We're just going to have to wait and see what transpires.'

Tamsin, who had overheard the conversation, wondered what her aunt meant about The Chocolate House, which was a relatively new venture — Vicki and Bruce's pride and joy. Tamsin knew that Vicki wasn't likely to confide in her.

She looked across at her cousin, who was immaculately-attired as usual; her make-up perfect in spite of the early hour. She couldn't have been more different from Tamsin, who was wearing her usual scruffy jeans and sweatshirt, thick fair hair tied back anyhow from her heart-shaped face.

The little group accompanied Alec and Cathy outside. Cathy got into the passenger seat and everyone waited patiently whilst Alec checked the boot for the hundredth time.

'Just making sure we've packed our wellies and waterproofs. It gets muddy on that farm.'

'Oh, you've no need to look for them. I put them in myself.' Charlie straightened the cover over the luggage. 'You look as if you've got everything but the kitchen sink in there, but I'm sure Uncle Sam and Aunt Sheila will lend you anything you've forgotten. Now, be off with you and leave the rest of us in peace!'

Alec jokingly made to cuff his son

and the others laughed. Charlie was head and shoulders taller than his father, and broader. He took after the Laceys, his mother's side of the family.

Alec finally got into the car. 'Ready?' he asked Cathy.

Cathy swept back her rather unruly brown hair, brindled with grey, which she'd jokingly remarked saved her a mint of money on highlights. 'Yes, I'm about as ready as I'll ever be, Alec.'

Tamsin smiled as her uncle said softly, 'Just untie those apron strings, Cathy. Our young people can fend for themselves. You're like a mother hen clucking over them.'

The trio of young people standing outside the rambling old house waved as the car pulled away. Tamsin knew that her Uncle Alec was itching to get back to his native Norfolk. He'd never understood her aunt's passion for Kent.

Cathy was a home-bird, never happier than when she was fussing over her family; but now that her father, Tamsin's beloved Grandpa Jim, had died, she no longer had any excuse for not accompanying Alec when he visited his brother and sister-in-law.

'Right,' Vicki said, looking at her brother and cousin, 'now, it's down to us to see that we keep everything running smoothly whilst they're away. Any problems — come straight to me, and don't phone Mum and Dad. They really need this break — understood?'

Charlie frowned at his sister. 'In Dad's absence, I'm the head of the family,' he informed her.

Vicki laughed. 'In your dreams. You also happen to be the youngest and least experienced!'

Tamsin didn't say anything. She'd lived with the Lambournes since she was ten, when her father had been killed in a tragic accident on an oil rig, and loved them to bits. Her mother, a nurse, had eventually remarried — a doctor in the hospital she'd been working in. She and Tamsin's step-father, Hugh, lived in Africa, so she rarely saw them.

Back inside the house, Tamsin began to clear away the breakfast things. Aunt Cathy had left her in charge of Lambourne Caterers and she was determined not to let her down.

★   ★   ★

The following morning, Tamsin had an unexpected visit from Lambourne Caterers' chef, Harvey Saunders. She was stunned when he placed his letter of resignation on the table, informing her that he and his wife were off to Devonshire to join his daughter and son-in-law, who had recently taken over a small hotel.

He assured Tamsin that he'd already prepared most of the food in advance for Lisa Clancy's wedding on Saturday, and that everything was ready for the dinner party that evening, although he wasn't able to help out at either function. Apparently he'd been working flat out, and everything was labelled and in the freezer.

When Harvey had gone, Tamsin made herself a coffee and took it into the office, wondering how on earth they were going to manage without him. Her Aunt Cathy was always singing his praises, saying what an excellent chef he was — if a little temperamental!

Tamsin bit her lip. She couldn't phone Charlie until lunchtime, and Vicki had already told her she was far too busy running The Chocolate House and looking after her young family to help out that evening.

A sudden hammering on the door brought Tamsin to her feet. Charlie's girlfriend was standing on the step looking anxious.

'Marissa! Whatever's the matter?' Tamsin asked in concern.

Marissa flicked back her unruly dark curls. 'You'll never believe what I've just heard about Harvey!'

'Yes I would, because he's just been here. Come on in — it must be your lunch break. I'll put the kettle on.'

Tamsin ushered her into the kitchen

and switched the kettle on, glad of the younger girl's company. Besides working part-time in the evenings for Lambourne Caterers, Marissa had a daytime job in a boutique.

'OK, so how did you find out?' Tamsin asked a few minutes later, handing her a mug of coffee.

Marissa perched on a stool, fished a packet of sandwiches out of her bag and bit into one of them hungrily. 'I bumped into Harvey's neighbour, Mavis,' she said between mouthfuls.

'Right! What a pity Harvey didn't think to mention his plans earlier! Well, we're in a bit of a fix, aren't we? Any suggestions?'

Marissa thought for a moment and then suddenly brightened up. 'There's always my mum. She loves cooking and she's helped out several times before when Mrs Lambourne's been stuck.'

Tamsin punched the air in relief. 'Marissa, do you think she would? I mean, she leads such a busy life.'

Marissa grinned. 'Well, my gran

always says: if you want a job doing, ask a busy person. To be honest, Mum could do with a bit of spare cash. Dad's not got so much work coming in these days. Shall I ask her, then?'

A surge of relief flooded through Tamsin as she thought of Pauline Wise, who was such a capable, friendly lady. 'Oh, yes, please. If you really think she can fit it in. You're a lifesaver, Marissa! But I must stress it's only on a temporary basis to start with — just until Aunt Cathy and Uncle Alec return.'

Luckily, Marissa managed to get hold of Pauline on her mobile. 'Oh, that's great, Mum!' She gave Tamsin a thumbs-up sign. 'Mum says sorry, she can't manage this evening, but she'd be delighted to help out at future events.'

Tamsin felt as if a great weight had been lifted from her. She hoped Aunt Cathy would think she'd made the right decision in inviting Pauline to join their team; but, after all, Harvey had assured Tamsin he'd already prepared most of the dishes for the forthcoming functions.

Tamsin owed her Aunt Cathy and Uncle Alec so much, and wanted to help out all she could now she'd got the opportunity. Years back, when her mother and Hugh had decided to work in Africa, they'd asked the Lambournes if they could continue to look after Tamsin, as where they were going wasn't the right environment for a girl of her age and they didn't want to disrupt her education.

Tamsin saw her mother and step-father periodically, but considered the Lambournes to be her real family now. They had supported her through her schooling and business studies course. She'd found an excellent job in the Midlands with a firm of auctioneers.

Three years back, however, when Tamsin's grandfather had become increasingly ill, she had offered to return to Kent to help look after him and lend a hand generally, so that Aunt Cathy could continue with her catering business. A short while later, Alec was made redundant; but by that time, Tamsin had proved herself to be almost indispensable.

Presently, Tamsin set out for the cash-and-carry armed with a lengthy list. Although Lambourne Caterers ordered the bulk of their provisions online, it was still necessary for her to do a certain amount of shopping.

A short while later, deep in thought, she wheeled her laden trolley between parked cars and crashed into someone coming from the opposite direction.

'Women drivers!'

'An apology would be good!' Tamsin retorted, nursing her wrist which was stinging, and glaring at the man. He met her gaze with a pair of amused, deep-blue eyes, which contrasted surprisingly with his thick, dark-brown hair.

'Actually, it was hardly my fault, as you weren't looking where you were going . . . What's wrong?' he enquired, seeing her wince.

'It's nothing — I caught my wrist on the trolley when we collided.'

Before Tamsin could protest, he had taken her hand in an unexpectedly gentle manner. 'Hmm — just a graze. Don't worry, you'll live. I've got a first aid box in the van.'

'Don't bother,' she told him, jerking her hand away. 'I've got one in mine, too.'

'Right — then I'll leave you to it.' And he wheeled his trolley towards a white delivery van with a distinctive orange and purple logo advertising CLANCY'S CHOCOLATES, leaving Tamsin staring after his retreating back. Fleetingly, she remembered the touch of his cool, comforting fingers encircling her wrist.

Gerald Clancy had a handmade-chocolate factory on the outskirts of the small town of Stanfield, and supplied The Chocolate House. Tamsin wasn't sure how she'd describe the man she'd just bumped into — tall and slim with rich dark hair and the deepest blue eyes. He was very different from Clancy's regular local delivery driver — much younger for a start. Tamsin grinned as she thought of Ray, who was bald, portly and had a florid complexion.

She put a spurt on. The jobs wouldn't get done if she stood there day-dreaming!

The day seemed destined to be on a collision course after that. Charlie, who'd agreed to help out at the dinner party, was late getting home from his job at the pharmacy. By the time they'd finished loading up the van Marissa had arrived; but there was still no sign of Angie, the fourth member of their team, and she wasn't answering her mobile.

Tamsin made a snap decision. She'd just have to wait behind for Angie, who needed a lift, and follow on in Charlie's car.

A short while later, a frantic call from Marissa sent Tamsin scurrying into the kitchen. In their haste to pack the van they'd managed to leave one of the main course containers behind. Tamsin had just located it when the phone rang again.

'Tamsin, I am so sorry,' came Angie's fraught voice. 'I'm afraid the baby-sitter's let me down and there's absolutely no-one else I can ask at such short notice.'

'I've got the same problem,' Tamsin told her frostily. 'Harvey's left us in the lurch and I've already had to rope Charlie in to help. Sorry, Angie — got to go. I'm running late as it is.'

The moment the words were out of her mouth, Tamsin regretted being so abrupt. Angie was a single mum with a six-year-old daughter; Tamsin knew she wouldn't have let them down if she could possibly have avoided it.

The wrought-iron gates to Lavender Lodge were flung wide open and, as Tamsin drove the short distance along the drive to the back of the charming, red-brick house, she began to relax. After all, Georgina Kershaw was one of their most regular clients, and such a dear that she was hardly likely to make a fuss if they were a little late.

Charlie came rushing out to greet her, fair hair awry. 'Thank goodness, Tamsin! The guests finished their starters ten minutes ago, and the fellow who's acting as host this evening is champing at the bit.'

'What are you talking about?' she demanded, struggling with the heavy container. 'Where's Mrs Kershaw?'

Charlie took the container from her. 'Apparently, she's been called away to a sick friend, and the man deputising for her isn't the most patient of individuals.'

Tamsin hadn't time to puzzle over this remark for, as she entered the beautifully-appointed kitchen, Marissa looked up from the stove in a panic. 'Where's Angie? This sauce is in serious danger of curdling!'

Tamsin flung off her jacket and leapt to the girl's side. 'Angie's had to call off. I'll sort this out. You concentrate on serving up. Let's go!'

Fortunately, the main course passed without any further mishaps. When it came to the dessert, however, a red-faced Marissa came dashing back into the kitchen. 'Quick, Tam, give me a cloth! I've managed to drop one of the mousses on the carpet!'

Tamsin's mouth twitched as she surveyed her young friend. 'I wondered what caused that loud burst of laughter just now. We'll have to start charging extra for the entertainment!'

Up until then, Tamsin had stayed in the kitchen, but now she volunteered to serve the coffee in the sitting-room whilst Marissa and Charlie cleared away in the dining-room.

Tamsin knew most of the guests, who greeted her in a friendly fashion. She was just about to hand Dr Avery his coffee when an all-too-familiar voice behind her said, 'Hallo, Tam. Long time no see!', causing her to slop the liquid into the saucer. The tall, sandy-haired young man grinned and rescued the cup from her.

Tamsin mumbled a greeting and pulled herself together with an effort. Dr Avery's son, Rob, was the last person she'd expected to see that evening! A real blast from the past!

'Lovely meal, Tam. Pity Mrs Kershaw wasn't here to enjoy it, eh, Fraser?'

Up until then, Tamsin hadn't paid any attention to the man standing by Rob's side; but now, with a start of recognition, she met the piercing blue eyes of the stranger she'd collided with that morning!

'I take my coffee black, thanks,' he told Tamsin, 'and preferably in the cup. Did you bring any petits fours or mints?'

She swallowed. Oh, no! Surely he wasn't the person acting as host that evening! What an unfortunate coincidence! Cheeks flaming, she murmured, 'Both actually, I'll fetch them,' and, avoiding Rob's amused gaze, she fled to the sanctuary of the kitchen.

'Charlie — who the heck's that guy

— the one who seems to be running the show tonight?' she demanded.

Charlie shrugged. 'Haven't a clue. Didn't catch his name. Can't say I've ever set eyes on him before this evening. All I know is, Mrs Kershaw wanted things to carry on as normal in her absence — typical Mrs K. Don't look so worried, Tam. The food was superb in spite of the glitches. There've been enough compliments flying around.'

'Well, that's something, I suppose.' She indicated the laden plates of petits fours. 'Can you take those in and see if any more coffee's needed? I don't think I can face that guy again. And then the pair of you had better get off home. I'll see to the rest of the clearing up.'

* * *

Tamsin surveyed the chaos surrounding her. The kitchen was still in a deplorable state and it was almost eleven o'clock. So far as she was concerned, the dinner party had turned out to be a complete nightmare, and seeing Rob Avery again after all this time had stirred up memories she'd prefer to forget.

She sighed as she filled the washing-up bowl with soapy water and tackled the glasses. Some years back, while they were still at school, she and Rob had gone out together. He'd been her first love and promised he'd always be faithful to her. She'd naively believed him; but, within a few months of going to medical school, he'd met someone else.

After they'd split up, Tamsin had only caught the occasional glimpse of Rob when he'd been visiting his parents, but each time it had felt like a stab to her heart. The last she'd heard, he'd become engaged to a young doctor called Zoe.

The door crashed open and an icy voice demanded, 'Why on earth are you still here? Don't you dare put those

20

plates in the dishwasher! They're irreplaceable — far too delicate. They'll have to be hand-washed.'

Tamsin and the man called Fraser glared at each other and, not for the first time that evening, she heartily wished she'd never set foot in Lavender Lodge that evening. She crossed to the sink and placed the plates carefully in the washing-up bowl.

'Yes, I'm well-acquainted with Mrs Kershaw's dinner service after the number of functions I've helped out at, and I've no intention of . . .'

She trailed off. Fraser had removed his jacket and pushed back his cuffs. Before she knew what was happening, he'd caught her round the waist and moved her smartly from her position in front of the sink.

'Budge up. The sooner we get this mess cleaned up, the sooner we can get to our beds; and if I'm going to help, then I prefer to wash.'

Tamsin gaped at him, her pulse racing from his touch. She knew she ought to be grateful for his help but she was tired and dishevelled and his presence unnerved her.

'That's better,' he told her presently. 'I'm afraid I can't say it's been a pleasure doing business with you, but it's certainly been an experience. This dinner party has been the biggest fiasco I could ever have imagined!'

Tamsin gasped and then said meekly, 'Well, I can only apologise if you were dissatisfied, but unfortunately there were extenuating circumstances, Mr, er — Fraser. If you'd just let me explain . . . '

He waved her explanations aside impatiently. 'Don't bother; it'd only inflame the situation so far as I'm concerned. I was led to understand that Lambourne Caterers was a thoroughly reliable company, but I have to say I've been disappointed.'

'It wasn't . . . ' Tamsin bit her lip. It was obviously no use attempting to explain to this arrogant, disparaging man that it hadn't been anyone's fault — just a series of disasters that had made Lambourne Caterers appear so incompetent.

Tamsin was far too weary to stand her ground. She didn't even know who this man Fraser was. She was tempted to point out that — even if things had gone a bit haywire — there had been plenty of compliments from the other guests. She swept up the bulk of the debris into a black plastic sack. Fortunately, Charlie and Marissa had taken the larger containers away with them.

Finally, Tamsin was ready to leave. She reached for her jacket, uncomfortably aware that the so-called host was waiting to escort her to the door. To her astonishment, as she made to leave he put a detaining hand on her arm.

'There is just one more thing before you go . . . '

A little shiver ran along her spine. His midnight-blue eyes seemed to mesmerize her, making her feel vulnerable, and she wished he'd remove his hand. She swallowed. 'Yes?'

'Why do you keep referring to me as *Mr Fraser*? It makes me feel like a character out of Dickens.'

'But I thought that was your name,' Tamsin said, puzzled.

Realising from her expression that the young woman standing in front of him hadn't got a clue as to who he was, he said, 'Well, yes, but most people would just say *Fraser*, or . . . '

The phone rang, leaving his sentence unfinished, and Tamsin took the opportunity to beat a hasty retreat. As she drove home, she found it difficult to get Fraser out of her mind. She was intrigued to know his identity, and couldn't understand how he'd come to be acting as host that evening. He certainly had a sharp tongue, and wasn't particularly good-looking — apart from those deepblue eyes that seemed to have a magnetic quality — but she had to admit there was something about him that had captured her interest.

★ ★ ★

It was the early hours of the morning before Fraser got to bed. He found himself thinking about Tamsin, wondering what on earth possessed her to work such unsocial hours. She'd looked pale and worn-out. He chuckled, acknowledging that the glitches had somehow added to the evening.

Perhaps he'd been a bit unreasonable. The food had been excellent, even if the service was abysmal; in the circumstances, he supposed the dinner party had really gone quite well. The guests had certainly been very complimentary and he'd made a few useful contacts. Oh, well, if the young woman was one of the Lambournes he was bound to encounter her again before long, now that he was working for Gerald Clancy.

2

The White Hart was crowded the following evening. Charlie and Marissa had persuaded Tamsin to join them for a drink. Marissa marched on ahead and then gestured at them to follow; rounding a corner, they saw Rob Avery, sitting on his own in an alcove. He beckoned to them

'That's convenient,' Charlie said, making his way towards him.

Tamsin caught hold of Charlie's sleeve. 'You've set this up, haven't you?' she whispered furiously.

'Well, you can't avoid Rob for ever — not now he's moved back to Stanfield. He came into the pharmacy this morning, so I invited him to join us this evening.'

Charlie took her arm firmly and guided her to Rob's side.

When Marissa and Charlie had gone

to the bar to get the drinks in, Rob turned to Tamsin. 'I've missed you, Tam.'

'It would be good if only I could believe that,' she told him with feeling.

He grimaced. 'Ouch! I suppose I deserved that. If only I could turn the clock back, Tam — with hindsight . . . '

'Yes, we could all say that,' she told him curtly. 'What about Zoe?'

Rob looked surprised. 'Didn't Charlie tell you? Zoe and I have split up. She's a lovely girl, but so ambitious. She's a complete workaholic — got a job in the States now.'

He hesitated. 'Look, the thing is, Tam, I've just moved back to Stanfield, and I was wondering if you'd come out to dinner with me one night — for old time's sake.'

Tamsin gasped. 'Are you serious? Surely you don't think I'd want to resume our relationship after all these years? You dumped me — if you remember.'

Rob caught her hands between his

and said softly, 'I'm truly sorry if I hurt you back then, Tam; but we were both teenagers, and, well, we've done a lot of growing up since, haven't we? I just thought it would be good if we could meet up for the occasional drink or meal, as friends, no strings attached.'

Tamsin looked at Rob across the table. He still had the same boyish good looks; sandy hair flopping over his forehead and such a winning smile. Her heart hammered and, with difficulty, she took a grip on herself. How easy it would be for her to fall for him all over again.

She told herself she had absolutely no intention of making the same mistake twice, but just the occasional night out couldn't do any harm, could it? She couldn't remember the last time she'd been wined and dined. Yes, that would be nice.

She smiled back. 'OK — but just meeting up as friends once in a while — is that understood?'

He squeezed her hand. 'Absolutely.

I'll look forward to that.'

To her relief, Charlie and Marissa appeared with the drinks at that moment.

'So are you back living with your parents, Rob?' Charlie asked.

Rob sipped his beer. 'Yes, just until I find a place of my own. I'll probably need to rent to begin with — so if any of you hear of anything, let me know.'

'Will do — so do I take it you'll be working in your father's medical practice?'

'Nothing's been decided yet,' Rob said dismissively.

Tamsin thought he seemed reluctant to discuss it and wondered why.

Charlie wasn't exactly renowned for his tact, but he intercepted Marissa's warning glance, took the hint, and didn't pursue it. The conversation inevitably turned to the previous evening's dinner party and the man who had hosted it.

'We still don't know who he is. Charlie turned up late and was busy

29

unloading the van so he didn't catch what the guy said,' Marissa told Rob.

Rob's eyes widened. 'He's Georgina Kershaw's son.'

There was a stunned silence and then Charlie exclaimed incredulously, 'But I didn't even know Mrs Kershaw had a son!'

'Well, it's hardly a state secret. Aunt Cathy's mentioned it on more than one occasion,' Tamsin told him. 'He lives in Somerset, so it just didn't occur to me that that's who he was. It's a pity you weren't listening when he introduced himself last night.'

Charlie shrugged. 'To be honest, Tam, I was concentrating on what I was doing and wasn't paying too much attention.'

Recovering from her initial surprise, Tamsin suddenly saw the funny side of things and laughingly recounted the conversation between Fraser Kershaw and herself the previous evening.

'No wonder he couldn't make out why I kept addressing him as *Mr*

Fraser, and the phone rang before he had the chance to put me right.'

'So how come he's been keeping such a low profile?' Charlie asked when the laughter had subsided. 'Mrs Kershaw must have been living at Lavender Lodge for at least a couple of years, and we've not set eyes on him before.'

Rob helped himself to some crisps. 'Actually, Georgina's only been there for eighteen months. Apparently Fraser has made the occasional flying visit to see her, but until recently he's been based in the Bristol area, where he's had a high-powered job in marketing, so she's mainly been to see him there.'

At least Fraser Kershaw had had the decency to support his mother when she most needed him, thought Tamsin.

Charlie swallowed a mouthful of beer. 'It seems like Mrs K's been in Stanfield forever, because she's fitted in so well and is such a sociable lady.'

The others agreed. 'I remember my mum saying Mrs Kershaw moved to Lavender Lodge from Somerset soon after her husband died,' Marissa added.

Rob nodded. 'That's right, and now that the company who employed Fraser has closed their branch in Bristol, he's come back to his roots too and is planning to stay around here for a bit.'

Tamsin set down her wine glass with a splash. 'How d'you mean — *he's come back to his roots?*' she demanded.

'He was born here in Stanfield. The Kershaws only moved away when he was around seven or eight.'

Marissa looked surprised. 'I didn't realise Mrs Kershaw had lived here before, did you, Tam?'

'Actually, yes. Apparently she knew our grandparents from way back, which was why she was so good about visiting Grandpa Jim, but I'd assumed she'd lived here before she'd got married.'

Charlie turned to Rob. 'So, what's Fraser Kershaw planning to do? I noticed he was deep in conversation with your Uncle Gerald last night.'

Rob studied his beer mat. 'Yes, apparently Fraser's been asked to do some marketing for Clancy's chocolate products.'

Tamsin snapped her fingers. 'I saw him driving one of Clancy's delivery vans yesterday.'

Rob nodded. 'He was covering for Ray who needed some time off to attend to a family matter.'

So that explained it, Tamsin thought. 'Right — I remember Aunt Cathy telling me once that Mrs K was related to the Clancys by marriage . . . '

She trailed off as Charlie interrupted, 'Doesn't that make him your cousin, Rob?'

Rob nodded again and cupped his hands round his glass. 'Sort of. My mother is Uncle Gerald's sister, but Fraser's father, Gil Kershaw, was their half-brother. My grandmother had been married before, you see. Gil was the black sheep of the family — moseyed off to do his own thing, leaving Uncle Gerald to take over the running of the business . . . Not that it made any difference. Can you believe that Gil inherited Lavender Lodge when his mother died?'

Charlie whistled. 'Really? I thought Mrs K bought it off that American couple who'd been living there.'

'No, actually they'd been renting it off Uncle Gil all that time. My parents tried to buy it off him, but he was a bit of a dog in the manger — didn't want to live there, but didn't want to sell.'

Rob paused and then added with feeling, 'Anyway, Fraser's back on the scene now, and he certainly hasn't wasted any time getting a foothold round here, has he?'

Tamsin thought she detected a trace of bitterness in Rob's tone and wondered why.

'You seemed to be getting on OK last night,' Charlie commented.

Rob shrugged. 'Oh, I'm sure he's a perfectly nice guy, but he and I have very little in common. I'm a people person — have to be in my profession — and, obviously, he deals with commodities in his line of business.'

'Well, I'm sure you both work equally hard, whatever you do,' Tamsin pointed out rather sharply, surprising herself by sticking up for Fraser Kershaw. She was still reeling from the surprise of discovering his identity and annoyed with herself that it hadn't occurred to her before. Her cheeks burned as she remembered the things he'd said to her.

The conversation moved on to more general topics. 'My mother was telling me about this café your sister and brother-in-law have opened, Charlie,' Rob said. 'I'm intrigued to know more — where exactly is it?'

'Vicki and Bruce have taken over Grandpa Jim's old place in Stanfield,' Charlie told him. 'D'you remember The Old Tea Shop? It had been standing empty for a while. Anyway, they've been quite enterprising by turning it into The Chocolate House — especially with Gerald Clancy's factory so close that they can promote local products.'

Tamsin smiled as Charlie enthused about The Chocolate House, explaining to Rob about the café adjoining a small shop that sold anything and everything to do with chocolate — from mugs advertising it to elaborate selection boxes.

'They make hot chocolate to die for!' Marissa added.

Rob looked amused. 'Well, then, you'd better make sure Vicki's got my father's phone number. Sounds like he might be picking up a few patients!'

Everyone laughed and Tamsin realised how much she'd missed Rob's quirky sense of humour. 'Seriously though, Rob,' she said, 'you ought to take a look for yourself some time. The café's not just for chocoholics. At lunchtime, there's homemade soup, salad, and a range of wholesome sandwiches and baguettes to choose from. The chocolate items are available for dessert and to accompany morning drinks and afternoon teas — mouthwateringly delicious cakes, ice-creams, mousses, etcetera.'

Rob licked his lips comically. 'Sounds

tempting! I might just call in some time and suss it out.'

'Why don't you? I'm sure Vicki would be pleased to see you.'

Presently, as they left the pub, Rob took Tamsin's arm. 'So when shall we make that dinner date?'

'Oh, I'm afraid it can't be until my aunt and uncle get back from their holiday,' she told him; and then, seeing his disappointed look, added, 'You could always drop by for a coffee, Rob.'

Tamsin knew that she was playing for time because, deep down, she still wasn't sure if she wanted to go out with him. Perhaps she'd been too hasty in accepting his invitation.

*   *   *

The following morning, Tamsin went to The Chocolate House to see her cousin. Stanfield was a busy little market town. The business was situated halfway along a passageway in a tall, narrow, red-brick building which had provided a home and livelihood for several generations of Laceys.

Vicki Miles looked up as Tamsin entered the café. 'Hi, Tam, I was just about to give you a ring. I expect you've come to collect the desserts for the dinner party this evening?'

Tamsin nodded. 'Yes, and to check that the chocolate fountain is organised for Saturday's wedding. Your mother phoned earlier wanting to know how things were, would you believe?'

Vicki frowned. 'She's supposed to be relaxing. I hope you managed to reassure her.'

Tamsin took a deep breath. 'I did my best — although I had to be a bit economical with the truth. She won't be happy when she finds out Harvey's left us in the lurch.'

'Harvey's what? What's happened, Tam?' Vicki leant across the counter, ignoring a couple of customers who were choosing cakes. 'You two haven't had words, have you?'

'No, absolutely not!' Tamsin assured

her indignantly. 'Look, any chance of you taking a break for ten minutes?'

Vicki had a quick word with her young assistant, Kelly, then removed her pristine tabard and smoothed her already-immaculate cap of blonde hair.

A few minutes later, Tamsin sat facing her cousin at a corner table with steaming mugs of hot chocolate and chocolate muffins in front of them. Once again, Tamsin relayed what had happened regarding Harvey.

Vicki clapped her hands to her head. 'That's all Mum needs! Well, surely he won't leave until after Lisa Clancy's wedding?'

'He already has,' Tamsin told her. 'He did a lot of overtime in lieu of notice.'

Vicki's face was a picture. 'Are you telling me he wasn't around for Mrs Kershaw's dinner party?'

Tamsin nodded. '*And* Angie had to cry off because of babysitter problems.'

Vicki gasped. 'So what happened? Why on earth didn't you ring me?'

'Because I knew you were busy.'

'Yes, but I'd have organised something. After all, I *am* head of the family while Mum's away, and she'd have expected me to help out in an emergency.'

'We coped,' Tamsin assured her. 'Charlie helped out — actually, Mrs Kershaw wasn't there.'

Vicki looked puzzled for a moment. 'But how could she have a dinner party if she wasn't there?' And then her face cleared. 'You're kidding me, aren't you? Mrs K cancelled, didn't she?'

Tamsin shook her head. 'No, her son, Fraser, acted as host for the evening.'

Startled, Vicki dropped her teaspoon with a clatter. After a moment, she said slowly, 'Fraser Kershaw is here in Stanfield?'

'Yes. Apparently, he's working for Gerald Clancy; and, what's more, Rob Avery's back in the area too.'

But Vicki didn't appear to be listening. She seemed to be lost in her own thoughts and Tamsin wondered if it had something to do with the problem Aunt Cathy had mentioned. To Tamsin's mind, her cousin didn't seem her usual self.

'Are the children all right?' she asked casually.

'Yes, fine, apart from Lucy having a slight snuffle, but Charlie suggested a magic remedy that helped her to sleep last night . . . OK, Georgina Kershaw's dinner party is out of the way and the one at the Cliffords' this evening is straightforward enough, but Lisa Clancy's wedding — that's a very different matter, isn't it? Mum said it's been such an enormous outlay. I know she was given a substantial deposit, but if anything should go wrong . . . '

'It won't,' Tamsin said, crossing her fingers behind her back. 'The Clancys were at Mrs Kershaw's dinner party and they would have said if there were any last-minute hitches, wouldn't they?'

'Hopefully. Right — let's hope to goodness we really are on top of things. From what I understand, Lambourne Caterers can't afford for anything else to go wrong. Mum says the business has existed very much hand-to-mouth recently.'

Tamsin's eyes widened. 'I, er, hadn't realised she'd discussed it with you.'

Vicki's eyes flashed. 'Why wouldn't she? I'm her daughter.'

Tamsin nodded. 'Yes, well, in keeping with a number of other smaller ventures, there have been signs that the recession is biting. It's nothing drastic.'

'Hmm.' Vicki didn't look convinced. 'Let's hope you're right. OK — to get back to the immediate problem. How are you proposing to manage without Harvey on Saturday?'

'Oh, he's left virtually everything ready in the freezer,' Tamsin said airily, trying to sound more confident than she felt.

'But there are always the finishing touches, and things that can't be done until the last moment.'

Tamsin sipped her hot chocolate. 'Yes, but it's nothing we can't handle, Vicki. Everything's under control. We'll cook the chicken pieces, and prepare the dips together with the salads, early on Saturday morning. The only things we've had to farm out are the bread rolls. Granted, there are the tables to lay up, but you're coming to lend a hand, aren't you?'

Vicki broke off a piece of muffin. 'Well, yes, but I wasn't planning on being there all day. Saturdays can be manic here.'

'Mmm, well, not to worry. We'll cope fine.'

Vicki was blissfully unaware of the problems Lambourne Caterers had encountered at Lavender Lodge, or that Tamsin had employed Pauline Wise on a temporary basis. Tamsin drank some more hot chocolate and reflected that Aunt Cathy had left her in charge, and so she must sort things out as she saw fit.

'Are there any more flapjacks, Vicki?' Kelly called out, causing a welcome diversion.

'Yes, I baked another batch yesterday.

They're out the back — second shelf down.' Vicki got to her feet. 'Right — let's hope things don't get too out of hand before Mum and Dad return! Lambourne Caterers can't afford for anything else to go wrong.'

* * *

On her way home, Tamsin made a detour and called into the local farm shop to check out the salad order for Saturday. She had been at school with Sue Morgan, who ran the shop with her husband Danny, and they had remained friends ever since.

'Turn the sign round, Tam. I'm going to close up for half an hour. Danny's helping his father this morning and I'm due a break.'

After going over the order, the two young women spent a pleasant time catching up on gossip over mugs of tea. 'Is it true Rob Avery's back in Stanfield?' Sue asked, head on one side.

Tamsin nodded. 'Don't look at me

like that, Sue! That was ages ago. I've grown up since then.'

Sue grinned. 'Hmm. Well, they say you never forget your first love, and you two were inseparable the summer before he went off to study medicine. It's not as if you've had a serious relationship since, is it?'

Tamsin coloured and decided not to mention that she'd already met up with Rob the previous evening.

Just as she was about to leave the shop, someone rattled the door handle impatiently. Tamsin turned the sign to OPEN and released the bolts. She stepped back, but not quickly enough. The door opened abruptly, almost flattening her against a stand of dried fruit.

'Oh, it's you!' came a voice she was beginning to recognise. Fraser Kershaw leant across her and deftly extracted a couple of packets of apricots that had sprung off and landed amongst the cauliflowers. 'Are you accident-prone, or what?' he demanded.

'Me?' Tamsin squeaked indignantly, conscious of the close proximity of this man. She caught a waft of his spicy cologne. His arm brushed hers as he straightened up, making her catch her breath. He grinned at her discomfiture.

'This reminds me of that game children played in a bygone era — sardines,' he said softly against her ear.

Tamsin was only too aware of Sue's interested gaze.

'Good afternoon, Mr Kershaw. I've got your mother's order ready for you,' she called out now. 'We'll have to move that stand. People keep cannoning into it . . . Have you got a shopping bag?'

Much to Tamsin's amusement, Fraser produced a capacious, bright red shopper with a flourish.

Sue chuckled. 'Well, you won't lose that in a hurry . . . Does your mother want any cherries? Danny's just picked some of those luscious black ones — very large and juicy.'

'Then I'd better take a pound.'

Tamsin tried to edge round him, and with a grin, Fraser moved out of her way. She grabbed her shopping and, mumbling a goodbye, hurried from the shop.

Outside, she encountered Danny trundling a laden wheelbarrow, and stopped to have a word with him. Sonny, the elderly Border Collie, greeted her affectionately and she stooped to pat him. From the corner of her eye, she saw Fraser leave the shop with a couple of laden bags and waited for him to go past, but he paused as Sonny ambled across to him.

Setting down his bags, Fraser hunkered down to stroke the animal.

'Fraser, have you met Tamsin Lacey?' Danny enquired.

'Yes — we, er, keep bumping into one another,' Fraser told him, a slight smile playing about his lips. He got to his feet and picked up the bags.

'Will we be seeing you at the meeting

on Monday?' Danny asked now.

'You certainly will, my mother and I are looking forward to it — thanks for reminding me.'

Danny turned to Tamsin. 'Mrs Kershaw's keen to join the Postcard Society. You ought to come along, Tamsin. Fraser's found a wonderful collection of albums at Lavender Lodge, and several of the postcards feature The Old Tea Shop.'

'Really? I'll bear it in mind.' Tamsin was surprised that Fraser Kershaw would be interested in local history. She was intrigued to hear about the postcards.

Danny's father called to him from one of the outbuildings and Tamsin began to walk towards the van. Fraser's shiny red Peugeot was parked alongside. Tamsin hesitated until he caught up with her. There was something she needed to know.

'How's Mrs Kershaw?'

His face took on a sombre expression. 'I'm afraid her friend died, so she's not feeling too bright just now.'

'I'm so sorry,' Tamsin sympathised. 'Please give her my condolences. It was good of her to continue with the dinner party in the circumstances.'

Fraser nodded. 'She didn't want to cancel at the eleventh hour and, as I was available, it seemed the obvious solution for me to act as host.' He looked at her quizzically. 'You might have known my mother's friend — Ellen Morris.'

Tamsin shook her head. 'No, I don't think so, although I might have known her by sight if she visited The Chocolate House.'

Fraser was more than a little surprised that she hadn't heard of Ellen. 'Somehow I don't think that would have been her scene, but I expect your grandfather would have known her.'

She nodded. 'Oh, yes, Grandpa Jim knew most people round here and he had the sort of memory that didn't forget a face.'

'Sounded a character — so you're interested in local history?' he prompted.

'Yes, I'm interested in anything connected with The Chocolate House premises. The building has been connected with my family for generations. More recently it used to belong to my grandparents, and was then known as The Old Tea Shop. My grandparents lived in the flat, over the top of it, for many years.'

Fraser smiled at her. 'Is that so? Then you must certainly take a look at those postcards some time.'

'That would be good. Things are very different now in Stanfield. There are a lot more shops and offices for one thing, but The Chocolate House has retained the original character of The Old Tea Shop and there's no possibility of it being spoilt.'

Fraser had his own reasons for being interested in The Chocolate House's premises. 'Is it a listed building?' he wanted to know.

'Unfortunately not, but it will never be pulled down — not if my family have anything to do with it!' she told him emphatically.

'Well, I suppose there are advantages of it not being listed. As I'm sure you're aware, there are very strict regulations regarding listed buildings which would have caused all sorts of complications for your family.'

She considered this. 'Yes, I suppose so. Well, at least they've been spared that.'

Fraser gave her a curious glance. 'You know, up until now, I quite thought you were one of the Lambournes.'

'Cathy and Alec Lambourne are my aunt and uncle, but they're away at present. Charlie Lambourne — their son and my cousin — was there on Tuesday night.'

So she was Neil Lacey's daughter. Well, well! Fraser looked thoughtful.

'Look, about the other night . . . ' Tamsin began awkwardly.

There was a slight twinkle in his blue

51

eyes. 'I think the less said about that the better, don't you? Now, if you'll excuse me, I've got a busy schedule.' And, clicking open the door, he climbed into his car and drove off.

3

Much to Tamsin's relief, the dinner party for eight that evening to celebrate a seventieth birthday went like clockwork. Pauline proved her worth in gold. She was a fast learner and, although a little too generous with the portions, soon got the hang of things.

'I've really enjoyed myself tonight,' Pauline said as they packed away.

'You did well,' Marissa assured her mother. 'Good on yer, Mum.'

'Yes, thanks so much,' Tamsin told her. 'You've fitted in remarkably well; hasn't she, Angie?'

Angie, the fourth member of their team, looked up with a grin. 'Yes, it's been great. Sometimes Harvey could be — well, just a little too serious about things.'

Tamsin nodded. 'Yes, but the fact remains that he was an excellent chef, and without his expertise, Lambourne Caterers might not function so easily in the future.'

'Oh, my mum and Cathy are pretty good cooks too, so I'm sure we'll manage,' Marissa said confidently, and Tamsin hoped she was right.

* * *

Friday was manic as Lambourne Caterers got everything ready for Lisa Clancy's wedding reception.

By three o'clock the following afternoon everything had come together. Tamsin stood alongside the rest of the team admiring the finished effect.

'Well, I think everything looks beautiful,' she remarked, surveying the peach-and-cream cloths and the arrangements of miniature roses matching the drapes on the inside of the marquee.

'It's awesome,' Marissa agreed, 'but I never thought we'd be ready on time. Yesterday there seemed to be the most unbelievable amount of things to do.'

'Oh, I knew it would all come together in the end, and your mother's been a wonderful help,' Tamsin told her, not admitting that she'd had a restless night imagining all the things that might go wrong. She'd finally fallen into a fitful sleep, and dreamt it had rained so hard that the marquee flooded and all the food was washed away!

'Let's be thankful we're only responsible for the food,' she added with a grin.

The floral table decorations, drinks and wedding cake were in the hands of others. The downside of this, however, had been that during the morning everyone had been milling about getting in each other's way, and there had been a great deal of tutting and muttering beneath breaths.

As soon as the guests began to arrive drinks were served by the wine waiters, and Lambourne Caterers sprang into action with a variety of hot platters of canapés. It was a sumptuous buffet with multitudes of pies and tartlets; mountains of different meat and fish dishes; and a selection of cheeses. There were large quantities of salads and miniature rolls from the bakery.

Lambourne Caterers stood to attention behind the tables, serving when required and making polite remarks when spoken to.

Much to Tamsin's relief, Mrs Clancy beamed her approval. 'This is absolutely magnificent, my dear. Your aunt would be so proud of you.'

'Well, I have to confess that Vicki's provided the vegetarian and vegan selection — in addition to the gâteaux. She always likes to emphasise that The Chocolate House serves healthy sandwiches, besides so many wonderful treats.'

Drusilla nodded. 'I did so enjoy Georgina Kershaw's dinner party too; although it was such a pity she couldn't be there herself. You've obviously had a busy week.'

'That's how we like it,' Tamsin assured her with a smile.

Drusilla Clancy turned away to greet some more guests just as Rob Avery crossed the marquee to Tamsin's table.

'Fantastic spread, Tamsin,' he said, piling his plate. Setting it down, he reached across the table and took hold of her hand. 'What a pity we can't escape from all this. It's far too sunny an afternoon to be cooped up inside.'

Tamsin pulled her hand away and busied herself serving one of the small bridesmaids who wanted to know if there was going to be any pudding. The little girl's eyes widened as Tamsin not only reeled off half a dozen desserts, but also promised to make sure she had a chocolate mousse *and* would be first in line for the chocolate fountain, after the bride and groom.

When Tamsin glanced up she saw Rob still standing there, talking to one of the other guests. She had to admit he looked devastatingly handsome in his dark suit; his sandy hair had golden flecks in it. He caught her gaze and smiled, and she coloured.

'You look equally as lovely in that uniform as all those girls in their fancy expensive outfits, Tam.'

Her cheeks flamed. 'Don't be ridiculous, Rob,' she chided, remembering his smooth tongue of old.

'We'll go out on that dinner date very soon,' he murmured *sotto voce*, and winked at her before picking up his laden plate and moving away.

Tamsin was just serving an elderly gentleman with a further helping of Caribbean chicken and rice when she realised someone was watching her. Passing back the plate, she glanced round and saw Fraser Kershaw surveying her coolly.

'I hadn't realised you were responsible for the catering. I have to say you've made a good job of it.'

Tamsin's cheeks were tinged with colour as she replied softly, 'Don't sound so surprised. I admit Tuesday wasn't up to our usual standard, but hopefully we've earned a reprieve this afternoon. Now, what can I get you?'

'Nothing. I've eaten, thanks — I was at the other end of the marquee. No, I just came over to congratulate you on behalf of my mother,' he added, meeting her surprised gaze.

'Oh, is Mrs Kershaw here?'

'Obviously, or she wouldn't have sampled the buffet.'

To her annoyance, Charlie chuckled; ignoring them both, Tamsin turned to help a lady struggling to reach the cold beef.

Presently, Fraser moved away from the table, leaving Tamsin to watch him unobtrusively. He was impeccably dressed in a silver-grey suit with a crisp white shirt and pale-blue silk cravat beneath. His rich dark hair was brushed back smoothly from an intelligent face.

He didn't have the conventional good looks of Rob Avery, but she had to admit there was something about his lean features and expressive dark-blue eyes that she might have found attractive, had it not been for his barbed tongue.

When everyone had eaten their fill, Tamsin and her team made short work of clearing the tables to make room for the champagne and wedding cake.

It was when the team were having a much-needed breather in the garden during the speeches and toasts that Vicki suddenly asked, 'D'you know who that man is with Georgina Kershaw, Charlie?'

Charlie grinned. 'You're not the only one who's been asking that question, Vicki. He's Mrs K's son, Fraser.'

As Charlie launched into an edited account of the dinner party, Tamsin suddenly noticed how pale Vicki was looking. Once or twice she rubbed her forehead. 'Are you OK, Vicki?' Tamsin whispered anxiously.

'Yes, of course — why wouldn't I be?' Vicki asked sharply, and then admitted, 'Actually, I've got a slight headache, Tam.'

But Tamsin wondered if that really

was all that was the matter. Vicki just wasn't her usual self.

Shortly afterwards they all trooped back into the marquee, where Vicki rose to the occasion and cut up the wedding cake, and served countless cups of tea and coffee. Presently the bride and groom, Lisa and Dominic, came over to have a word with Lambourne Caterers, and the team offered their congratulations.

'What a wonderful dress,' Marissa said dreamily as Lisa floated away in a cloud of satin and lace. Tamsin smiled at her young helper, realising she must be wondering if Charlie would ever get around to proposing to her. As for herself, Tamsin did not even allow herself to dream these days.

★　★　★

A smiling Mrs Clancy came across to Tamsin as she was preparing to leave. 'I wanted to thank you once again for all your hard work, my dear. You and your team have come up trumps and those desserts Victoria provided were to die for. She's such a talented young woman, as I was just saying to Fraser Kershaw. You met him on Tuesday evening at Georgina's dinner party, didn't you? Come to think of it, I haven't seen Georgina recently. She was looking very tired earlier on.'

Tamsin looked around the marquee. 'Oh, I can see her. She's over there with her son, and . . . ' She trailed off as she noticed the pretty young brunette sitting next to Fraser Kershaw.

Mrs Clancy followed Tamsin's gaze. 'So she is . . . oh, good! Petrina's with them. I thought poor Fraser might feel a bit left out of it. He knows hardly anyone here. Anyway, I had a sudden inspiration and introduced him to my niece, Petrina, because she's just started work in the office in our factory and Fraser's doing some work for us, too.'

Fraser was listening attentively to something the young woman beside him was saying. Tamsin felt sure he could be charming when he chose and, just for an instant, wondered what it would be like to exchange places with Petrina.

'Did you hear where Lisa and Dominic have gone on their honeymoon?' Mrs Clancy enquired, cutting across Tamsin's thoughts.

Tamsin shook her head, and after a significant pause Drusilla said, 'Bali — I've always wanted to go there, but Gerald's never wanted to travel beyond Europe.'

There had been a time, before Grandpa Jim had become so ill, that Tamsin had decided to see something of the world, she thought wistfully, but it wasn't to be.

Some of the guests came to speak to Drusilla Clancy, and Tamsin took it as a signal to leave before she and her team were delayed any further. She'd arranged to clear away the remains of the buffet the following morning, leaving covered plates of food in case anyone felt peckish.

The others had gone on ahead, and Tamsin was just about to climb into the van when she spotted Georgina Kershaw sitting on a seat overlooking the lily pond and went to have a word with her.

'Hello, Mrs Kershaw. It's been a lovely day, hasn't it?'

Georgina Kershaw smiled and smoothed the pleats of her lavender silk dress. 'Yes, Lisa made a beautiful bride. It was getting a bit hot in the marquee, so I thought I'd leave the young people to themselves for a little while, and come out here to have a breath of fresh air. I could really do with going home, but I'm not sure if my son is ready to leave.'

'I could take you, if not,' Tamsin volunteered. 'That's if you don't mind a ride in the van.'

'Oh, I don't want to put you to any trouble, dear, but if you're sure.'

'Absolutely . . . I was so sorry to hear about your friend.'

Georgina's expression was sad as she

stared into the lily pond. 'Yes, Ellen was an old school chum. She was matron of honour at my wedding to Gil. It doesn't seem five minutes ago when we were exchanging girly secrets, but time marches on. She had been ill for some time, but the end was rapid. Anyway, I'm pleased to hear the dinner party was such a success on Tuesday.'

'Well, actually, I'm afraid there were one or two hitches,' Tamsin confessed.

The older woman smiled. 'Yes, dear, Marissa told me. What on earth are you going to do without Harvey?'

'Oh, I guess we'll manage somehow. Anyway, I'm afraid that's Aunt Cathy's problem, although, in the short term, I've hired Pauline Wise.'

Georgina chuckled. 'Yes, she's an absolute hoot, isn't she? She kept us entertained all afternoon. Such a cheerful soul and good at her work.'

Tamsin bit her lip. She'd have to have a quiet word with Pauline about not being too familiar with the guests.

Some people mightn't be as tolerant as Mrs Kershaw.

Georgina secured her hat more firmly on her neat, brown hair. 'If you're not doing anything tomorrow afternoon, Tamsin, perhaps you'd like to have a cup of tea with me — around fourish? I haven't settled your bill yet.'

There were a dozen things that Tamsin needed to do the following afternoon, but she decided they could wait. 'Yes that would be lovely, Mrs Kershaw. Look, in view of all the glitches, we'll knock off 10%. I'm sure that's what Aunt Cathy would expect.'

'Nonsense! I tell you what, how about bringing one of Vicki's gorgeous cakes to go with our tea, and we'll call it quits. I think Fraser was being over-conscientious.'

As if on cue, a now-familiar voice said, 'Ah, here you are, Mother. I wondered where you'd got to. Are you ready to go home now?'

'Yes, Fraser. I've been ready for the past half hour, but don't feel you've got to leave on my account. Tamsin's offered me a lift.'

He raised his eyebrows. 'In the van?'

'Well, of course — where's Petrina?'

'Oh, Warren Clancy's introduced her to a distant cousin with a daughter about her age. I'm quite ready to leave now so your lift won't be needed, Miss, er, Lacey, but thanks anyway.' He took his mother's arm. 'Shall we go and say our goodbyes?'

Georgina smiled apologetically at Tamsin. 'It looks as if I'll have to wait for a ride in your van for another day. When are Cathy and Alec due back from their holiday?'

'Not until next Saturday.'

Georgina turned to Fraser. 'Tamsin's in a bit of a predicament. She's holding the fort whilst her aunt and uncle are away, but unfortunately, their chef's walked out. Usually, Tamsin only helps out when an extra pair of hands is needed; otherwise she's behind the scenes sorting out the business side of things, aren't you, dear?'

Tamsin nodded, uncomfortably aware of Fraser Kershaw's dark-blue eyes surveying her. She mumbled a hasty goodbye and hurried over to the van.

★   ★   ★

The following morning, many hands made light work clearing up after the wedding. It seemed the party had gone on rather longer than the Clancys had anticipated.

Gerald Clancy handed Tamsin an envelope containing a cheque for the buffet together with a generous tip in cash. 'You've done us proud, Tamsin. Your aunt and uncle will be so pleased to know how well things went in their absence,' he told her, shaking her hand warmly.

Tamsin passed on his compliments to her team, and told them they'd be receiving overtime and a tip along with their wages.

As soon as they'd completed their tasks, Charlie drove Tamsin and Marissa to Vicki and Bruce's home. They'd been invited to Sunday lunch which was to be a barbecue.

The modern semi-detached house where Vicki and her family now lived was a complete contrast from the flat above The Chocolate House where she and Bruce had spent the first two years of their married life.

When they arrived, Vicki was in the kitchen making a salad and, much to Tamsin's relief, seemed very much her usual self. 'Tam, can you finish this salad whilst I decorate the trifle?' she asked briskly. 'Charlie, do go and help Bruce with the barbecue or we'll never get any food. Marissa, can you catch the children and get them to wash their hands?'

As Tamsin began to slice the cucumber, she looked across the neat garden where two small figures were haring round a tree and smiled. Vicki was blessed with such gorgeous children. Not for the first time, Tamsin felt a slight pang of envy.

Vicki reached for the cherries. 'How many functions have you got between now and my parents' return?'

'Three, but fortunately, they're very straightforward,' Tamsin informed her. 'There's the over-sixties luncheon club — that's just a roast and apple pie. Harvey's left a stack of his fruit pies in the freezer. And then on Wednesday there's a dinner party at The Grange, but only for six and nothing elaborate. Friday there's an eighteenth birthday party for around forty in the church hall — just the usual young people's buffet; again, nothing fancy. Actually, they could probably have done it themselves by shopping at the supermarket.'

Vicki frowned. 'Well, don't tell them that! What about the vegetarian choices for these events? Have you thought those through? If you run into problems you'd better get in touch — although I'd appreciate a bit of advance notice.'

Tamsin assured her cousin that she and the team had everything in hand.

Vicki was so efficient, she found it difficult to accept that other people were perfectly capable of organising things, too.

'I wish you'd consulted me before you employed Pauline Wise. Goodness alone knows what my mother's going to say about that!'

'Pauline's a perfectly capable lady, and I'm sure Aunt Cathy will be more than happy that she's agreed to help out. We were in a tight spot,' Tamsin said firmly.

As Vicki covered a trifle with cling film she suddenly said, 'I hear Robert Avery's come back to live in Stanfield. I gather he and Zoe have parted company. Just a word of warning, Tamsin: I sincerely hope you're not going to throw yourself at him again. The pair of you were very young before — you were still at school and he was just about to begin his medical training. It was just a silly schoolgirl crush, as I remember it.'

The colour stained Tamsin's cheeks.

Rob had sworn his eternal love for her and she had been devastated when he had transferred his affections to someone else. She counted up to ten under her breath before saying calmly, 'Oh, I'm a lot older and wiser since those days, Vicki . . . Now, what else is there to do?'

Vicki checked the jacket potatoes. 'That's about it, thanks. I hope those men hurry up and get that barbecue going or these'll be overdone. I've cooked the chicken drumsticks already.'

She perched on a stool. 'There's nothing would make me happier than seeing you settled with the right partner, Tam.' She hesitated and then, looking her cousin up and down, added, 'You know, you could do with a bit of a makeover. I could give you a few tips if you like.'

Tamsin swallowed. When she'd found her voice she said sweetly, 'Thanks Vicki, but actually, I thought the creased look was rather fashionable just now. Anyway, it isn't really necessary to dress up for a barbecue in the garden, is it?'

Vicki was prevented from replying by the timely intervention of her husband who appeared in the doorway and gave them the thumbs-up sign.

'Reporting that the barbie's fully operational and the sausages and burgers are sizzling. What's up? You two are looking serious.'

Tamsin liked Bruce and had no intention of ruining the occasion. 'Oh, just girly chatter, that's all,' she said lightly. 'Could you take this bowl of salad out with you?'

To give Vicki her due, the meal was everything it should be and, even though it was a barbecue, a table was set up in the gazebo. The children — Lucy, aged three, and Jamie, who was two — behaved beautifully.

'I love dining alfresco,' Bruce announced, biting into a drumstick. 'So, what's this son of Georgina Kershaw's like? I couldn't get much out of Vicki.'

'That's because there was nothing

much to say,' Vicki told her husband.

'Well, I don't remember setting eyes on him before — not that I've set eyes on him now.'

Tamsin thought of Fraser Kershaw with his soft Somerset accent, dark hair and expressive eyes; and an inexplicable little shiver ran along her spine. She smiled wryly, realising that when it came to finding fault, he could run a close second to her cousin. Perhaps, like Vicki, he was a perfectionist.

'He's called Fraser and he's just started working for the Clancys,' Marissa offered.

'According to Rob Avery, he's in marketing,' Charlie put in. 'Perhaps he's going to work on some new promotions, take a fresh look at advertising — that sort of thing.'

Vicki paused in the act of cutting up a sausage for her small son. 'Well, let's hope he hasn't got too many highfalutin ideas.'

'But surely any promotions that boost sales can only be a positive thing, so why worry?' Tamsin remarked, helping herself to more salad.

Vicki pursed her lips but made no further comment. Tamsin thought there seemed to be a bit of an atmosphere, and again wondered if there was something going on concerning The Chocolate House that she wasn't being told about. It would certainly explain why Vicki was so tense.

* * *

'Come and see our vegetable patch, Tam,' Bruce invited presently, when everyone had helped to clear away. Marissa and Charlie were playing with the children whilst Vicki was sorting out a cake for Mrs Kershaw.

Bruce led the way to the bottom of the small garden and proudly pointed out the neat rows of onions, carrots and brassicas, which Tamsin duly admired.

'I've got Alec to thank for getting me started on this. He's trying to persuade me to have an allotment like him, but that needs real dedication.'

Tamsin laughed. 'Yes, I've realised *that*, since we've been keeping an eye on things whilst he's been away. Thank goodness it's rained once or twice to save on the watering . . . Bruce, is everything all right with Vicki?' she asked, as he stooped to examine his lettuces. 'I thought she's seemed a bit uptight just recently.'

'What? Oh, Vicki's just a bit tired and in need of a holiday, that's all.' He straightened up. 'The thing is, Tam, the business hasn't been doing as well as expected during the past months. We've put in the hours but it's been a disappointing return.'

Tamsin stared at him in disbelief. 'Really? But whenever I've gone in, there always seems to be a steady stream of customers — and Vicki says it can be manic on Saturdays.'

Bruce wiped his hands on his handkerchief. 'Yes, but a number of those customers are regulars. They sit nattering to their friends over a hot chocolate or cappuccino for about an hour. Our lunchtime trade has diminished and our orders for cakes have been slack. Between you and me, Vicki was grateful for the extra cash she earned from Lisa Clancy's wedding yesterday.'

Tamsin was taken aback. 'I'm sorry to hear all this, Bruce. I thought everything was fine with your business.'

He pulled up a couple of weeds. 'The recession has a lot to answer for. I'm afraid we're even considering cutting back Kelly's hours. We've already had to let our Saturday lad go and he wasn't best pleased.'

'Perhaps Fraser Kershaw could help, if he's so good at marketing,' Tamsin suggested

Bruce brightened. 'Yes, that would be great. We could certainly do with a fresh promotion, Tam, and if the Clancys are prepared to organise and finance it, then I'm all for it. We're prepared to give anything a go to increase our profits.'

He hesitated. 'But I'm afraid there

are other problems too, which I can't discuss at present.'

'Oh, dear, I'd no idea things were so bad,' Tamsin said sympathetically. She couldn't imagine what other problems there could be. No wonder her cousin seemed so tense just lately. Vicki and Bruce's livelihood was at stake, and they'd got two small children and a hefty mortgage.

Bruce placed a hand on Tamsin's shoulder. 'Not to worry. We'll come through. We're not going to give up that easily. Not when we've worked so hard to make The Chocolate House a viable business. Let's hope this is only a temporary blip. And, Tamsin, I'd appreciate it if we could keep this conversation between ourselves. Don't let on that I've told you, will you, or my name will be mud!'

'Discretion is my middle name,' she assured him, tapping her nose, 'but I'm glad you've confided in me. And, if there's anything I can do to help, just let me know.'

Presently, she went home to change before going to tea with Georgina Kershaw. Glancing at herself in the mirror, she had to admit that Vicki had had a point when she'd told her she needed to do something about her appearance. Her shoulder-length, fair hair could do with a trim, and her clothes had seen better days.

She thought of her promised dinner date with Rob Avery and grinned. It was high time she changed her image. She'd go on a shopping trip when her aunt and uncle returned from their holiday.

4

Tamsin rang the bell at Lavender Lodge and stood balancing the cake box carefully, as she waited for Georgina Kershaw to answer. She nearly dropped it when the door suddenly flew open and Fraser Kershaw stood there.

'Oh, it's you again,' he said.

'Yes, it's me — sorry to disappoint you, if you were expecting someone else.'

His blue eyes flickered. 'So, what can I do for you?'

'Fraser, is that Tamsin?' Georgina called out and she appeared behind him in the doorway. 'Well, don't keep the poor girl standing on the step. Come along in, dear. Oh, good, you've brought the cake. I forgot to mention to Fraser that you were coming to tea.'

Fraser stood aside and Tamsin reluctantly stepped into the hall and placed the cake on the table. She'd have thought up an excuse not to come if she'd known Fraser Kershaw was going to be there.

'Peace offering?' he enquired, *sotto voce*.

'Certainly not,' she whispered back indignantly, wishing she could beat a hasty retreat.

'Fraser, could you put the kettle on — oh, and find a plate for the cake, and the server. I've got a bit of business to do with Tamsin before tea . . . Come along into the study, dear.'

Tamsin did not dare to look at Fraser as she walked past him into the study.

Georgina had her chequebook out. 'Now, you haven't given me the bill, Tamsin, but Cathy quoted me a price before she went away, so if it's any more you must let me know.'

'Well, in view of what went wrong, perhaps we ought to leave it until Aunt Cathy gets back,' she suggested awkwardly.

'Nonsense! You know what I said

yesterday, and Fraser didn't mention anything too calamitous. You've brought a cake, so let that be an end to the matter.'

Fraser hadn't made a fuss after all? Tamsin couldn't believe her ears.

He was waiting for them in the sitting-room. 'I've made the tea and managed to find the cake server. It was wedged at the back of a drawer.'

'Oh, well done! I wondered what had happened to it. You can pour the tea, Fraser. Role reversal this afternoon; Tamsin must be tired of waiting on others.'

Fraser grinned and obediently poured the tea, handed it round and then offered the plate of scones. Tamsin suspected Georgina was doing her best to put her at her ease. She hadn't expected Fraser would be joining them for tea.

She was uncomfortably aware that, although she was wearing a clean skirt and top suitable for visiting Georgina Kershaw, she was hardly fashionable and must appear very much the country bumpkin as far as he was concerned.

'My son's going to be staying with me for a while — just until he finds a place of his own. Although, if he makes himself too indispensable, I might not want to let him go!'

Georgina kept the conversation flowing and, after they had discussed the wedding at some length, she said suddenly, 'I do miss your grandfather, Tamsin. It seems like only yesterday when I was popping in to your place for a cup of tea and a chat with him.'

Tamsin nodded. 'Yes, we all miss him dreadfully. He was such a lovely old gentleman.'

'So what do you do when you're not working?' Fraser asked during a lull in the conversation.

Tamsin was startled. It seemed a very long time since anyone had asked her that question. She swallowed her mouthful of scone. 'Oh, my work keeps me very occupied so I don't have much time for outside interests.'

'You're being far too modest, Tamsin,' Georgina said. 'Tamsin's a wizard at découpage. Her lovely cards sell in The Chocolate House and the church, as well as one or two other venues.'

'Really? I must look out for them,' Fraser said.

Georgina suddenly said, 'That reminds me, Tamsin, Fraser's going to be making an informal visit to The Chocolate House tomorrow morning. I'm afraid I've got a dental appointment in the opposite direction, and so I was wondering if you could show him where your cousins' café is. It's not the easiest place to find if you don't know your way around.'

Fraser looked as startled as Tamsin felt. She had countless things to do the following morning, but didn't like to refuse Mrs Kershaw's request, especially as she'd been so understanding about the dinner party.

'Well, I, er — yes, of course I will,' she floundered.

'Oh, I'm sure I don't need to bother Tamsin, Mother. The Clancys will explain where it is and, anyway, I've got the sat nav.'

'That doesn't help when it's a pedestrianised area,' Georgina pointed out. She had her own private reasons for wanting the two of them to be friends.

Fraser hesitated for a moment. 'Right — well, thanks then. I'll pick you up from your house at eleven o'clock — just in time for elevenses.'

'Is that all right, Tamsin?' Georgina enquired. 'I'm afraid Fraser's used to arranging appointments to suit him.'

Tamsin expected Fraser to give his mother a sharp reply, but instead he said mildly, 'If it isn't convenient, just give me some instructions, Tamsin, and I'll make my own way there. A café that's off the beaten track must be at a disadvantage.'

'Not at all. The locals know where it is and there's a board at both ends of the passageway.' She supposed the

85

Clancys wanted Fraser to become acquainted with the local businesses they supplied.

Georgina handed him the cake knife, and he cut the lemon drizzle cake with precision and served it expertly. 'Fraser did a stint as a waiter when he was a student and likes to keep his hand in.'

'So, if you hadn't been hosting the dinner party, you could have helped us out the other night,' Tamsin said, tongue-in-cheek, and saw the glint in his eyes.

Georgina laughed. 'You've met your match, Fraser. You two ought to have a lot in common. Tamsin's a very capable businesswoman, and I'm sure her aunt and uncle have found her skills invaluable.'

'Oh, it's only routine office work,' Tamsin murmured, embarrassed.

'Don't be so modest, Tamsin,' Georgina told her again. 'Your grandfather often said if it wasn't for you keeping an eye on the business side of things, your family would have been out of pocket on many an occasion.'

She turned to Fraser. 'As Alec Lambourne has frequently told me, the smooth running of the business is down to Tamsin. She deals with the accounts, and very often sorts out the orders with the customers over the phone, too.'

Tamsin coloured as she saw the keen look Fraser gave her.

'Are both your aunt and uncle involved in running Lambourne Caterers?' he asked.

'Uncle Alec enjoys his allotment and provides a lot of fresh vegetables for the catering business,' Tamsin explained. 'He's a dab hand at preparing them, too. He generally makes himself useful, and sometimes helps out in The Chocolate House, but it's Aunt Cathy who — up until now — has sorted out the menus with Harvey, and together they've experimented with new dishes.'

'Yes, everyone's going to miss Harvey.' Georgina set down her pastry fork. 'That cake is absolutely delicious — Victoria is such a talented young woman. She obviously takes after Cathy . . . Changing the subject, I've suddenly remembered something that might interest you, Tamsin. We're going to a meeting of the Postcard Society tomorrow evening.

'As you're probably aware, Danny Morgan is the chairman. We've lent him a couple of albums Fraser's just unearthed in the attic, so that he can do a bit of research, and he's going to project some of the postcards onto a screen for everyone to see. Perhaps you'd like to join us, Tamsin? It promises to be a good evening.'

Seeing Tamsin hesitate, she added persuasively, 'And then you could tell Cathy all about it. I'm sure she'd be most interested.'

Without knowing quite how it had happened, Tamsin found herself agreeing to go. 'It sounds fascinating! Actually, Danny Morgan mentioned the postcards when he was talking to us outside the farm shop on Thursday. I'd certainly be interested to see them. You know, I hadn't realised Lavender Lodge had belonged to the Clancys for all those years.'

'Oh, yes, it's got quite a chequered history. Fraser's grandmother, Charlotte Clancy, was married twice, you see. My husband, Gil, was her son from her first marriage to William Kershaw. William was a naval officer and was killed during the war. She married Matthew Clancy when Gil was about ten.

'Anyway, when she was widowed for the second time, she continued to live at Lavender Lodge and then, when she died, she left the place to Gil. Of course, it was rented out for a number of years before I came to live here.'

'So now you've been given a potted edition of our family history,' Fraser said, and his mother shot him a reproachful look.

'Well, I think it's all very interesting, and I'll enjoy seeing those postcards,' Tamsin told them.

'Good, then we'll need to sort out a time to collect you,' Georgina said with an air of satisfaction.

Fraser set down his plate. 'We'll make arrangements tomorrow morning when we go to The Chocolate House.'

Tamsin suddenly wondered if Bruce and Vicki were aware Fraser was planning to call on them the following morning. She decided to ring them when she got home, so that they were prepared for his visit.

As Fraser showed her out presently, he reached over and touched her arm, sending a little shiver trembling along her spine. 'Don't feel you've been press-ganged into going to the meeting tomorrow evening. If you'd rather not, I'll quite understand. Nor do you have to accompany me to The Chocolate House. I'm sure you've got better things to do, and someone at Clancy's will tell me where it is.'

'What makes you think I don't want to go to the meeting?' she asked with a little smile. 'I'm keen to see those postcards and to hear what Danny's got to say about them. Your mother's particularly asked me to take you to The Chocolate House, and I've got no intention of letting her down. I'll see you tomorrow morning at eleven o'clock sharp.'

Tamsin did not wait for his reply. Fraser stood staring after her, a grin on his face. He admired her spirit and, although they'd got off to a bad start, he felt he'd like to get to know her better.

He decided she was really quite attractive, with her abundance of wavy fair hair, tied casually back from an oval face, lovely clear grey eyes and a creamy skin almost devoid of make-up. Pity about her dress sense, though — which was deplorable.

'Tamsin's a lovely girl, isn't she?' Georgina remarked when he joined her in the sitting-room. 'It would really please me if the two of you could be friends.'

Fraser placed a hand on her shoulder. 'Then I'll do my very best — just to please you,' he told her with a smile.

* * *

No sooner had Tamsin put down the phone from speaking with her cousin, than it rang. 'Hi, Tam, are you doing anything this evening?' came Rob's voice.

'Well, there's a good programme on TV I was planning to watch — why?'

Rob hesitated slightly and then said in a rush, 'Actually, Tamsin, I really need to speak to you before someone else does. There are things I need to tell you . . . can I call round about eightish?'

There was a pause. Tamsin's mind was working overtime as she wondered what on earth he wanted to tell her. 'OK,' she said at last. 'It'd be great to catch up over a coffee, but I've got an early start in the morning — as I expect you have — so I'm afraid I'll have to throw you out whilst the night's still young.'

Rob chuckled. 'Thanks for the warning — see you later. Oh, and I haven't forgotten that dinner date.'

'It hadn't even crossed my mind,' she assured him, 'but, just for the record, I haven't actually accepted.'

* * *

Rob was punctual. 'Hi, Tam,' he greeted her and gave her a hug. 'I like that top you're wearing!'

Tamsin ignored this remark, determined to let him see that she would not be easily won over by compliments. She hadn't made a point of dressing up for Rob, but had changed into a fairly respectable pair of black trousers and a coral-coloured over-blouse.

'Come along into the sitting-room. I still can't get my head round you being back in Stanfield.'

'I can assure you it's me in person and not a cardboard cut-out,' he said humorously.

Tamsin busied herself in the kitchen,

pouring the coffee and arranging some biscuits on a plate. She was feeling rather nervous. When she brought in the loaded tray, she found Rob studying a photograph on the unit. 'Charlie's graduation,' she informed him unnecessarily.

He took the tray from her. 'He's done well for himself, hasn't he? He was telling me about his job in the pharmacy.'

Tamsin nodded and handed him the coffee. 'Yes, he really enjoys working there. Help yourself to cream and sugar. Oh, and these chocolate biscuits from Clancy's are something special. We have to save them for high days and holidays.'

His green eyes met hers in an intense stare. 'And is this a high day, Tamsin?'

'Don't kid yourself!' she said lightly. 'Now, what is it you wanted to tell me that's so important, and how did you know I'd be on my own?'

'I ran into Pauline Wise at the

newsagent's this morning. She mentioned that Charlie and Marissa were going to hers for supper this evening — so I thought now would be a good opportunity to come to see you.'

'Right — so, come on, Dr Avery, what is it that you're burning to tell me?'

Rob, who had always been so self-confident, seemed on edge. He twisted his hands in his lap and suddenly blurted out, 'Actually, Tamsin — I'm not . . .'

Tamsin frowned. 'Not what? Rob, I don't think I've ever known you lost for words before. You're usually so full of confidence.'

He sighed. 'I'm not a qualified doctor. I dropped out of med school before I took my finals — so now you know!'

Tamsin stared at him, open-mouthed. 'But what about your dream of becoming a GP?'

He spread his hands. 'It was just that — a dream. As time went on, it became increasingly clear that I was going along the wrong path. It's probably a blessing in disguise. I'd have made a lousy doctor!'

Tamsin was silent, finding it difficult to take on board what he was telling her. She sipped her coffee, trying to think of something to say. At last she looked up.

'I'd no idea, Rob. Your parents haven't let on. They were over the moon when you graduated.'

He helped himself to another chocolate biscuit. 'Yes, at least I had the sense to work until I'd got a degree under my belt. That's got to count for something — when I can establish what I want to do. The problem started when I resumed my medical training after the degree course. I'm afraid I spent too much time having a good time.'

Tamsin looked at him in amazement. 'Rob, you've just told me you've thrown your career away, and you don't seem that bothered.'

He shrugged. 'It wasn't to be, so better I found out sooner rather than later.'

There was a pause, and then Tamsin asked, 'So what have you been doing with yourself all this time?'

'My parents took my decision to drop out very badly, and I'm afraid we had a bit of a bust-up. Anyway, I went off travelling round the world, doing a bit of work to pay my way. I had a whale of a time. I don't regret it one little bit. And now the prodigal son has returned, and I'm footloose and fancy-free once again.'

His eyes met hers briefly, but Tamsin chose to ignore this comment.

'So what now? I mean I quite thought you'd be working in your father's practice.'

Rob gave her a wry smile. 'No way! He's trying to persuade me to look at other options linked to the medical profession. Eventually, I suppose I'll have to do some sort of retraining programme.'

'And in the short term?' she prompted.

He leant back in his chair. 'Oh, I'm

earning my keep. I've got a part-time job at a local nursing home, and I'm making myself useful at home. Gardening isn't my father's strong point and I like the great outdoors ... Anyway, enough of me — what's been going on in your life recently? The last I heard you were working for a firm of auctioneers in the Midlands.'

'Oh, there's nothing much to tell. When Grandpa Jim's health deteriorated, I came back here to help care for him and take over most of the office work, so that Aunt Cathy could continue with her catering business. Shortly afterwards, Uncle Alec was made redundant and it was important for him to get involved with Lambourne Caterers, because he was getting a bit down, so I stayed on.'

Rob looked indignant rather than sympathetic. 'So, what about you? Didn't anyone bother to find out what you wanted?'

'It was my choice to come back here,' she replied quietly. 'And I'm pleased I was able to spend some quality time with my grandfather. After all, I'm always going to be grateful for the way Aunt Cathy and Uncle Alec took me in when I was a child.'

His eyes narrowed. 'Well, isn't it time you did what you wanted for a change — went off to see something of the world, perhaps? I mean, couldn't you visit your mother and stepfather in Africa?'

'Yes, of course I could if I chose, but I'm happy enough here in Stanfield for the moment.'

'But you've had a taste of a different life. Don't you miss it?' he persisted. 'After all, you had your own home once, didn't you?'

'Goodness, no — I shared a rented flat with a couple of other girls. It was all right, I suppose, but hardly home. I liked my job well enough at the auctioneers'.'

Tamsin smiled as she thought briefly of big Terry, the auctioneer, and his son Callum. She'd gone out once or twice with Callum, but it hadn't been anything serious — just workmates socialising over a meal, and a mild flirtation. Yes, she had enjoyed those years, but it was true, she was happy enough in Stanfield; until someone like Rob made her feel she was missing out — and then she became restless.

She got to her feet. 'I'm going to make some fresh coffee. Fancy a sandwich?' She busied herself in the kitchen, mulling over all that Rob had said.

He suddenly appeared in the kitchen doorway and, as she looked at him, she felt her heart miss a beat. Just for a moment, it was as if the years in between had rolled away and they were teenagers again.

'I've never forgotten you, Tam,' he murmured softly, putting an arm around her shoulder and giving her a gentle kiss. 'And now I've returned to Stanfield, it's as if we've never been apart.'

Pulling herself together, Tamsin shook

off his arm. 'I find that difficult to believe, Rob,' she said unsteadily. Obviously, he thought she would provide a convenient stop-gap between relationships. Well, he'd got another think coming!

She realised Vicki was right about one thing. She would be foolish to get involved with Rob again, but when she looked at him, she knew it would be all too easy.

'So, when was the last time you and I met up, Rob?'

He looked startled. 'Last week in the pub,' he suggested.

'Oh, you know what I mean. I saw you at the carol service at Christmas, but you were at the other side of the church — that's how it's been all these years. You've avoided me every time you've been staying in Stanfield, and the only news I've received has been from your family.'

'Didn't you get my postcards from down under?'

' Yes, thanks, but I hardly think that counts. I think you'll agree, it's been out of sight, out of mind. I thought you were abroad doing part of your training, but now you've admitted you were off on your travels having a wonderful time.'

Rob had the grace to look abashed, but it was hard to remain cross with him for long. Soon he was telling her some amusing anecdotes of his travels: of the people he'd met and the sights he'd seen. The time shot past and they were both surprised when Charlie arrived home. Rob got to his feet.

'Throwing-out time, I think,' he jested. 'Thanks for this evening, Tam. I'll be in touch.'

She stood in the doorway waving goodbye. He hadn't kissed her again, apart from a light peck on the cheek. He'd hurt her badly all those years ago, and even after all that he'd said that evening, she still wasn't sure that she wanted to rekindle their relationship.

5

By eleven o'clock the following morning, Tamsin had managed to get through a fair number of chores, and had just tidied herself up when Fraser's car pulled up on the drive.

During the short drive into Stanfield, Tamsin was extremely conscious of the man sitting beside her. She could smell his cologne — fresh and tangy. She shot a surreptitious glance at him, registering the strong hands on the wheel, the tanned arms, and his slim but muscular frame. Did he work out? she wondered.

'Have you got any suggestion as to where I can park?' he asked, suddenly breaking into her thoughts. 'This one's full and we're in danger of holding up the traffic.'

Tamsin calmly directed him down a side street where she knew they could safely park for an hour or so.

'Right, so it's follow-my-leader from now on,' Fraser told her as he locked the car.

'It's only a few minutes' walk from here,' Tamsin assured him as he fell into step beside her.

They entered the high street of the small market town and Tamsin led him along a passageway sandwiched in between two buildings. Halfway along it widened out, and The Chocolate House with its bright orange awning and colourful hanging baskets came into view. She waved her hand in the general direction.

'Here we are — not too much off the beaten track, you see.'

'Wow! So this is The Chocolate House! Amazing! I'd never have expected to find it tucked away down here!'

Fraser stood still for a moment studying the building, an inscrutable expression on his face. 'It's certainly an interesting place. I can imagine what it must have been like years ago in its heyday as a tea shop! It's one thing looking at a postcard — but to see the real thing is so much better.'

Tamsin was pleased by his unexpected interest in a place that was so dear to her own heart. 'It was originally two separate shops. There used to be a draper's where the chocolate shop is now, but the original tea shop has belonged to my family for generations,' she told him proudly. 'It was known as The Old Tea Shop. The Laceys lived in the flat above it. Come along in and meet my cousin and her husband.'

Vicki was serving a customer when they entered The Chocolate House. Fraser looked about him, apparently taking in every detail — from the burnt orange walls above the wood panelling, adorned with prints of The Old Tea Shop, to the reproduction oak tables and chairs. Suddenly, Bruce appeared from the back of the shop and came to meet them.

Tamsin introduced the two men, and shortly afterwards Vicki joined them, leaving her young assistant Kelly in charge. For the next fifteen minutes they sat over coffee and chocolate flapjacks, making general conversation. Tamsin wondered what exactly the purpose of Fraser's visit was.

Presently, Vicki turned to Tamsin, looking slightly awkward. 'Tam — Fraser, Bruce and I have a few business matters to discuss, so if you'll excuse us . . . Kelly will get you another coffee. You're welcome to stay as long as you like.'

Embarrassed, Tamsin sprang to her feet. She ought to have realised whatever they wanted to discuss wasn't intended for her ears.

'Thanks for showing me the way,' Fraser said. 'I admit I would have had difficulty finding it by myself. If you want a lift back, I'll be about half an hour.'

'Thanks but, I've got rather a lot to do at home so I won't hang about,' she told him rather pettishly.

The bus went round the houses and Tamsin had plenty of time to wonder what Fraser needed to discuss with Vicki and Bruce. Surely there wasn't a problem concerning Clancy's factory? If Vicki and Bruce had got wind of that, then they would naturally be worried. They were dependent on Clancy's for the bulk of their products for The Chocolate House, and would have to do a lot of research to find another supplier of the same quality. After all, The Chocolate House was only a small enterprise, and some manufacturers only wanted to deal with large orders.

She hadn't been home more than half an hour when the phone rang.

'Tamsin, it's Bruce. Look, about this morning . . . '

'You've no need to explain, Bruce. You obviously had something of importance to discuss with Fraser.'

Bruce sighed. 'Not really. Thanks for tipping us off. He'd left us a message on the shop answerphone, telling us he was proposing to call in, but we didn't pick it up until this morning. Unfortunately, Vicki had got herself into a bit of a state by then, thinking he was coming to present us with some grandiose ideas for marketing Clancy's chocolate products, amongst other things. As it turned out, he wanted to discuss a totally different matter altogether . . . I suppose you had to get the bus home?'

'Yes — well, Fraser did try to tell me he'd find his own way to The Chocolate House, but Mrs Kershaw asked me to show him the way so that's exactly what I did.'

Bruce chuckled, 'So now he thinks you're the Blue Guide for Stanfield. Anyway, I'm going to leave it to Fraser to explain to you what his visit was about — part of it, anyway. Sorry for messing up your morning. Must go now, Vicki's signalling to me!'

Tamsin put the phone down feeling more mystified than ever, but placated by the call. Before she had a chance to mull over what Bruce had said, it rang again, and this time it was Fraser.

'Tamsin, I've rung up to apologise.

I'd no intention of leaving you stranded this morning.'

'You didn't,' she assured him. 'I chose to make my own way home rather than hang about.'

'Well, thanks for your help. We'll have a chat about the purpose for my visit sometime soon. Now, about this evening — shall I pick you up around seven?'

★ ★ ★

The Postcard Society met above a pub just off the high street. There were about fifteen members in the room that evening. Tamsin looked about her with interest, and Sue Morgan waved to her from her seat at the front.

'We've got a real treat tonight,' Danny told everyone at the start of the meeting. 'Fraser Kershaw has discovered three albums of postcards at Lavender Lodge and most of them are of Stanfield. It's a real find. Great to see you and Mrs Kershaw here tonight,

Fraser — and Tamsin Lacey, too.'

Danny was an interesting speaker. He had a knack of making the pictures come alive and Tamsin listened, fascinated.

Lavender Lodge featured on a number of the cards. Tamsin hadn't realised just how influential the Clancys had been in Stanfield. There were a series of pictures of the chocolate factory too, and then came the ones she'd been waiting for of The Old Tea Shop.

Some of them she'd seen before, but there were a number of new ones dating back to her great grandparents' time. She wondered what they would think of The Chocolate House. As if reading her mind, Fraser stole a glance at her.

'Riveting, aren't they?'

She agreed, and shortly afterwards, the lights came back on.

'We'll take a break now, everyone. Your drink orders should be ready — ah, here's Mollie, right on cue.'

During the break, everyone had the

opportunity to examine some of the postcards on display, and there were also some for sale. Tamsin noticed that some people were swapping cards too. Fraser fetched Tamsin and his mother their drinks.

'Oh, I'm so glad I came tonight,' Georgina Kershaw said. 'Danny is such a good speaker. I've learnt so much. Have you enjoyed it, Tamsin?'

'Absolutely. It's been fascinating. What a pity Aunt Cathy wasn't around. She'd have loved to have seen those postcards of The Old Tea Shop. There are several I've not seen before.'

'Well, I'll make sure she gets to see them,' Georgina assured her. 'Fraser, I fancy joining this society. Have you got any money on you?'

Fraser grinned and reached into his back pocket. 'Excuse us for a few minutes, Tamsin.'

Whilst they were gone, Sue came across to speak to Tamsin.

'What a nice surprise to see you here tonight, Tamsin. Do I take it you came with the Kershaws?'

'You do. Mrs Kershaw invited me.'

Sue gave her a meaningful look. 'Mmm — well, Fraser seems a nice chap. Related to the Clancys, isn't he?'

Tamsin jabbed her friend in the arm. 'You're outrageous, Sue! Stop reading things into situations. I had a lift — that's all.'

Sue laughed. 'Well, that's a start. I expect he enjoyed the buffet on Saturday. I gather the wedding went well. Seriously, Tam, It's good to see you taking time out. High time you did. Oh, Danny's beckoning to me. See you later.'

'Can I get you another drink?' Fraser asked, a moment later.

'Oh, no thanks.' Embarrassed, Tamsin wondered how long he'd been standing there.

'Well, I feel I know a lot more about Stanfield now. Danny's certainly done his research.'

'It's been great,' she told him simply. 'I'll have a lot to tell my aunt about. I was particularly interested to see that picture of your parents and my grandparents outside The Old Tea Shop.'

Fraser looked thoughtful. 'Yes, I expect it was a good photo opportunity, don't you?'

Tamsin wondered what he meant by the remark, but before she could say anything further they were asked to take their seats for the second half of the meeting.

As Fraser dropped Tamsin off outside her house, Mrs Kershaw said, 'I've thoroughly enjoyed myself this evening, Tamsin. Thank you for your company, dear.'

Fraser leant across to open Tamsin's door, brushing against her as he did so. It was as if an electric charge shot along her arm.

'I suspect we'll be making this a regular monthly outing, so if you fancy joining us next time . . . Oh, and I'll drop by some time to explain about this morning.'

It had been a good evening, Tamsin decided, pleased that she'd accepted the invitation. She'd been surprised to find how much she'd enjoyed Fraser's company.

★ ★ ★

On the following day, the monthly luncheon for the over-sixties club in the village hall was plain sailing. Pauline rose to the occasion admirably and the roast beef went down a treat. It was cooked to perfection: the roast potatoes were crispy, whilst the Yorkshires were like puffs of wind. The apple pie and custard was a triumph.

Fortunately, Harvey had left the pies ready in the freezer; no-one could make pastry like Harvey.

Pauline was in her element. She obviously knew a number of the elderly folk and they appreciated her banter. The downside was that Pauline had to rush off at two-thirty, which left Tamsin and Angie with the clearing-up to tackle. They both heaved a sigh of relief when the van was eventually loaded up. Only two more functions to go before Cathy and Alec Lambourne got back.

Charlie rushed home about six, showered, changed and grabbed a coffee before disappearing out again. Apparently, he and Marissa were meeting up with friends for a pizza in town.

'I wish you'd have told me earlier,' Tamsin said crossly. 'There's a steak and kidney pie in the oven.'

'Sorry, thought I did. I'll have it tomorrow.'

'I doubt that, it'll be dried up, and it's one of Harvey's too. Anyway, go and enjoy yourself and make sure you've got your key.'

Charlie pulled a face at her. 'You sound just like Mum. You'll be asking me if I've remembered to change my socks next!'

Tamsin had to laugh. He was irrepressible. How Aunt Cathy and Uncle Alec had come to have two such different children, she would never know.

Left alone once more, Tamsin decided to have an early supper and watch a DVD. She had prepared far too many vegetables but she'd put them to good use the following day. She was just about to serve up when the front door bell pealed.

To Tamsin's surprise, Fraser was standing on the step clutching a large brown envelope. 'I've had some copies made of those postcards of The Old Tea Shop — thought you might like them.'

'That's really kind — thanks.' She hesitated and then, as he made no attempt to move, asked, 'Would you like to come in for a coffee?'

She stood aside and he stepped into the hall. 'If you'd like to go into the sitting-room, I'll just turn the oven down.'

To her embarrassment he followed her into the kitchen. He sniffed appreciatively. 'Something smells good

— your supper?'

She nodded. 'I was just about to eat, actually.'

'Well, I don't want to spoil your meal. My mother's out this evening and I've told her I'd grab something at the pub. I don't suppose — no, that would be too much to ask . . . '

Tamsin stared at him. 'Are you hinting that you'd like to stay for supper?'

He smiled at her. 'Have I made it that obvious?'

She nodded. 'It was quite a strong hint.'

He chuckled. 'I gather I'd be helping your cousin out of a hole.'

'How d'you make that out?'

'I met him on the drive just now. He said he was in the dog-house as you'd over-catered.'

Tamsin was amused, but tried not to show it. 'You're right. Charlie forgot to tell me he was eating out tonight so there's plenty of food, but it's pretty basic. One of our previous chef's meat pies and plenty of fresh veg. If that'll do, I'll go and set the table.'

She made for the door, but he caught her arm. 'I don't want to put you to any trouble. Can't we eat in here?'

His fingers felt as though they were burning into her arm. Her pulse quickened. 'I'm not sure what my Aunt Cathy would have to say about that,' she said, taking a grip of herself. 'She's a stickler for etiquette and our guests don't usually eat in the kitchen.'

His eyes twinkled. 'Ah well, I'm not exactly a guest, am I? And I promise not to tell.'

Tamsin whipped out a tablecloth, found a couple of napkins and hurriedly set the table. 'Sit yourself down and then I can serve up. I'm afraid there's no starter.'

He laughed. 'Tamsin, you're trying too hard. Just be yourself. I may have been a little over-critical the other evening, but that was a very different situation.'

Her cheeks flamed, and she was

uncomfortably aware that those piercing blue eyes were watching her. She placed his meal in front of him. 'Help yourself to vegetables, gravy and horse-radish sauce. Would you like some fruit juice — or I think there's a beer in the fridge?'

'Sit down before your meal gets cold,' he commanded.

Ignoring him, Tamsin found a couple of glasses and placed the fruit juice and beer on the table.

He reached in his pocket and found a penknife with a bottle-opener attached. 'I used to be a Boy Scout,' he told her with a grin as he helped himself to a beer. 'Now, let me explain about yesterday morning, as Bruce and Vicki have left it to me to fill you in.'

'There's no need,' she said, cutting into her pie and hoping it wasn't over-cooked. Fortunately the pastry melted in her mouth and the meat was tender.

'Actually, I think there is. As you know, I'm staying with my mother, but that's only a short-term arrangement. In the meantime, I've been looking around for somewhere more permanent to live.'

Tamsin looked at him, puzzled, wondering what that had got to do with Vicki and Bruce. Surely they weren't planning to take in a lodger?

He poured his beer into a glass. 'Yesterday, I went to take a look at the flat above The Chocolate House.'

She frowned, trying to make sense of what he was saying. 'Surely you're not thinking of living there!'

'Got it in one! That's exactly what I'm doing. It's going to take a few weeks to sort the flat out, as it's been empty for so long and needs doing up, but it's quite roomy. At present, it's mainly used for storage, but with a bit of reorganisation, the back of the premises on the ground floor can be utilised more fully.'

'And Vicki and Bruce have agreed to that?' she asked incredulously, fork poised.

He looked amused. 'Well, of course. I could hardly move in without consulting them, could I?'

'I would have thought you'd have been a great deal more comfortable at Lavender Lodge with Mrs Kershaw.'

'But, if I get my feet too firmly under the table, I might not want to leave,' he pointed out reasonably. 'Anyway, I'll be staying at Lavender Lodge for a while yet, until I get things how I want them at the flat.'

Tamsin supposed Vicki and Bruce had come up with the idea of letting out the flat as a good way of supplementing their income, but it was all rather sudden and she was frankly amazed.

There were a number of questions Tamsin would have liked to ask the man sitting opposite her, but she didn't want to seem too inquisitive. After all, this was the first real opportunity she'd had to speak to him. He seemed to have no such reservations.

'So, what made you decide to work

for Lambourne Caterers?' he asked now. 'Bruce tells me you've got good business qualifications.'

'Oh, family matters brought me back here,' she said, and told him briefly about her grandfather.

Fraser looked thoughtful. 'Yes, my mother was very fond of your grandfather. They went back a long way.'

'It's strange, but I hadn't realised *that* until recently. Grandpa Jim didn't actually mention your family.'

Fraser realised he would have to be cautious about what he said. There were obviously things Tamsin wasn't aware of. 'Well, sometimes old friends come back on the scene after a number of years, and that's what happened when my mother returned to Stanfield. I understand she'd kept in touch all these years.'

Tamsin nodded, deciding she'd have to ask Aunt Cathy to fill her in. She was beginning to realise there was a lot she didn't know about her family.

'Would you like another slice of pie?'

she asked as he set down his knife and fork.

'Please, if it's going spare.' He handed her his plate. 'Didn't my mother tell me your chef was moving on?'

'Yes, he went to Devon at the weekend. My aunt and uncle aren't aware he's left yet.' She cut a generous portion of pie and handed back the plate. 'He put in lots of overtime and took unpaid leave in lieu of working his notice, which has rather left us in the lurch.'

Fraser helped himself to more vegetables. 'You seem to be coping.'

She looked at him in surprise. 'That's not what you said after the dinner party last week.'

He had the grace to look abashed. 'No, perhaps I was being a bit unfair. Looking at things from my angle, I was thrown in at the deep end with a number of people I hadn't met before. It was an unusual occasion, to say the very least.'

'It would have helped if I'd known who you were,' she told him, lifting her eyebrows skywards.

He laughed. 'Yes, in retrospect, I suppose it was quite amusing. Anyway, shall we start again? That was a thoroughly enjoyable meal.'

To his relief she seemed mollified.

'Good. So what would you like for dessert? I've got stewed fruit and custard or ice-cream — nothing more elaborate, I'm afraid.'

'Fruit and ice-cream will be fine.' He patted his stomach. 'I wasn't expecting dessert. The first course was very substantial.'

'Charlie has a very healthy appetite.'

After they'd finished eating, Tamsin insisted Fraser went into the sitting-room whilst she loaded the dishwasher and made the coffee.

Presently, when she took it in, she discovered him leafing through a brochure about Lambourne Caterers which she remembered had been on the coffee table, along with some music magazines of Charlie's and a card she was working on for Marissa's birthday. Setting down the tray, she scooped them aside.

'Your work?' he asked, studying the card.

She coloured. 'Yes, I enjoy messing about with bits of paper.'

'I should imagine it's therapeutic after working on accounts most of the day. Shall I pour?'

As they sat with their coffee, he indicated the brochure on his lap. 'You know, this brochure could do with being updated. Do you think Mr and Mrs Lambourne would be open to a few suggestions?'

Tamsin gaped at him, taken aback by his nerve. After a moment or two she said, 'I suppose you could always mention it, but Lambourne Caterers has gained a reputation mainly through word of mouth. It's only a small concern, and if my aunt and uncle started going heavily into marketing, then they'd have to up the prices to cover the costs.'

He nodded. 'Yes, of course. Forget it. I was only trying to be helpful.'

'And to put out some feelers for some freelance work, no doubt,' she said, grey eyes flashing. 'Now, if I remember rightly, you take your coffee black.'

'That depends on the occasion and whether I'm in danger of falling asleep,' he responded. 'Actually, I'd quite like some cream.'

Presently, he set down his cup and, reaching over, touched her arm. 'You're wrong, you know, about my motive for wanting to update this brochure. And just to prove it — I'll produce a new one for free to make up for my boorish behaviour when we first met.'

Her skin prickled beneath his touch. Before she could reply, the phone rang in the hall and, with a muttered apology, she hurried from the room.

It was Vicki, sounding worried. 'Tamsin, thank goodness you're there!

'Why, whatever's wrong?'

'Bruce has been in London all day. He rang about ten minutes ago to say his train's been cancelled, and now I've had a call to tell me one of The Chocolate House windows has been smashed. I've got to get down there, but I obviously can't leave the children, and . . . '

'I'll be straight there,' Tamsin promised and rushed back into the sitting-room.

'Sorry, Fraser, I've got to go out immediately. Vicki's got a bit of a crisis on her hands.'

She explained briefly and Fraser sprang to his feet. 'I'll come with you — give Vicki some support.'

When Fraser and Vicki had left for The Chocolate House, Tamsin checked on the children and picked up one of Vicki's glossy magazines, but found it difficult to concentrate. After what seemed like an age, Bruce arrived home. As soon as Tamsin had explained what had happened, he dashed back out again. Eventually, Vicki returned, looking white and strained.

'We could have done without that. Thank goodness Fraser was around. He's helping Bruce to board up the window.'

'Was there a lot of damage?' Tamsin asked, getting to her feet.

'No, thank goodness, but it's a pain. They've made off with several boxes of chocolates, but fortunately we'd emptied the till. Thanks for holding the fort, Tam.'

'I'll put the kettle on,' Tamsin said, trying to be practical. 'I expect you could do with a hot drink.'

'A camomile tea would be wonderful — how come Fraser was at yours?'

'Oh, he came to tell me about the flat and stayed for supper,' Tamsin called over her shoulder as she went into the kitchen. When she returned with the tea a few minutes later, Vicki was lying back with her eyes closed and her legs outstretched.

Tamsin would have liked to have asked her a few questions about Fraser renting the flat, but somehow it didn't seem appropriate, and she realised it would have to wait.

Eventually, the men returned, and Fraser drove Tamsin home. 'Well, that was an unexpected ending to the evening,' he commented. 'Does a lot of that sort of thing happen in Stanfield?'

'No more than anywhere else,' Tamsin said rather defensively. 'I'm sure Vicki and Bruce were grateful for your help.'

'Oh, it was the least I could do. Anyway, it's a good thing you were around to babysit. You're a close family, aren't you?'

'Yes, I suppose we are. Aunt Cathy and Uncle Alec have given me a home since I was about twelve, when my mother remarried.'

Shortly afterwards, they pulled up on the Lambournes' driveway, and Tamsin realised Charlie was home. She didn't invite Fraser to come inside again as it was getting late.

'Goodnight, Tamsin. Thanks for a

delightful meal,' he said, taking her hands between his for a moment, and a little shiver danced along her spine at the contact.

'You're welcome,' she told him lightly.

'We must do it again sometime — the other way round.'

Tamsin smiled as she let herself into the house. Life was full of surprises, and Fraser Kershaw was one of them. The more she got to know him, the more she found to like about him.

6

Much to Tamsin's relief, everything went smoothly for the remainder of the week. The dinner party on Wednesday evening was a great success, and the teenager's party was a complete doddle. Once Tamsin and her team had brought in the hot platters, they had nothing further to do and were able to leave.

On Saturday evening, Cathy and Alec Lambourne returned, looking completely relaxed and ready to take up the reins again — or so Tamsin thought.

'We've had a wonderful time,' Cathy told her son and niece. 'Norfolk is such a lovely county and we've really been able to unwind.'

It was after supper, when they were all enjoying a cup of coffee in the sitting-room, that Tamsin dropped the bombshell about Harvey. There was a silence, during which her aunt and uncle exchanged meaningful glances with one another.

'This could hardly have happened at a better time,' Alec said at last. 'In fact, it's providential.'

'How d'you mean, Dad?' Charlie asked, puzzled.

'Whilst we've been away, your mother and I have had plenty of time to discuss things. We're not getting any younger, and Lambourne Caterers has been very hard work recently. I expect you've noticed we're not exactly making a wonderful profit, Tam?'

'Well, yes,' Tamsin agreed, wondering what on earth Uncle Alec was about to tell them.

There was a slight pause and then, at a nod from her husband, Aunt Cathy said, 'Our visit to your Uncle Sam and Aunt Sheila set us thinking. Sam is in his element running that smallholding, and you know how your father enjoys his allotment, Charlie.'

'I'm not quite sure I follow this train

of thought,' Charlie said, looking mystified.

Alec Lambourne cleared his throat. 'In a nutshell, we've decided to give up the catering business and move to Norfolk.'

There was a stunned silence and then Charlie said, 'But what would you do for capital? I mean, neither of you are retirement age yet, and you can't live on fresh air.'

'Well, we're not entirely penniless, Charlie. We have got a bit put by for a rainy day, thanks to your grandfather. For the time being, just until the house is sold, we intend to move in with Sam and Sheila. Your dad's going to help Uncle Sam part-time, and I'm sure I can find something to do in the village — even if it's only on a voluntary basis to begin with.

'We were planning to downsize anyway and the property prices will, hopefully, be lower in Norfolk than here. Our living expenses would be cheaper there too.'

'I see,' Charlie said, studying his shoes. 'So Lambourne Caterers would just be dissolved?'

Cathy nodded. 'We did think of asking Harvey if he'd be interested in taking it over, but to be honest, we knew he wouldn't be able to raise the capital. Fortunately the problem's resolved itself for him, as he's found another job already.'

'So, what about Marissa and Angie?' Charlie demanded.

'Well, obviously we're sorry for them, but Marissa's got the job in the boutique and I'm sure Angie will be able to find something. They were both only part-timers anyway.'

Tamsin would never have believed in a million years that her aunt would have agreed to move away from Stanfield and her family. She saw the look of happiness on Uncle Alec's face, and realised that, as usual, her aunt was being selfless.

Having got over the initial shock, Tamsin kissed her aunt and hugged her uncle. 'If it's what you want to do, then I'm happy for you. It's lovely if you can follow your dream, but I'm not sure if I want to move to Norfolk.'

Uncle Alec slung an arm around her shoulder. 'We had a feeling you might say that, Tam. Now, we were wondering if this might be a golden opportunity for you to visit your mother and Hugh in Africa. You've been such a wonderful help to us that we're prepared to pay your fare as a thank-you.'

Tamsin swallowed. 'I don't know . . .' She sank onto a chair. It was suddenly too much for her to take on board.

Her aunt looked worried. 'Well, love, if you really want to stay on in Stanfield, you and Charlie could remain here until the house is sold — which could be several months with the way the market is — during which time, you'd have plenty of opportunity to find yourself more work and somewhere else to live.'

Charlie sprang to his feet. 'I'm going for a drink with Marissa. I'll let her know your news, shall I?' he asked stiffly.

'I'd rather you didn't just yet,' his mother told him. 'I realise it might be better coming from you, but we won't be going for a month or two yet, and we don't want any rumours flying about. We can't let any of our clients down; although we haven't taken any firm bookings too far ahead.'

Tamsin stood up too. 'I thought we hadn't got much custom beyond the next few weeks. This isn't a sudden decision, is it?'

Aunt Cathy appeared uncomfortable. 'No dear, but we weren't a hundred per cent sure until we'd discussed things with Sam and Sheila.'

Tamsin nodded. 'I'm going for a breath of fresh air. I'll see you presently.'

★   ★   ★

'Well, that went down like a lead balloon!' Alec remarked, as soon as

Tamsin and Charlie had left the room.

'And we haven't even told Vicki yet. I don't understand it. I thought Tamsin would have jumped at the chance of going to Africa,' Cathy said worriedly. 'I'm not so concerned for Charlie. He's got his job at the pharmacy and he's got Marissa, so I suspect he'll move in with the Wises. But what about Tamsin? She's dependent on us for work.'

Alec put a comforting arm about her shoulder. 'Oh, it'll all turn out all right, you'll see. Tamsin is a sensible girl. She probably just wants time to think things through. She's got good qualifications — thanks to us supporting her through her schooling and business studies course.'

Cathy frowned. 'I've heard Rob Avery is back in Stanfield — you don't suppose . . . ?'

Alec shook his head. 'Stop worrying. It'll all work out in the end, you'll see,' he said confidently, patting his wife's arm.

Charlie encountered Tamsin on the upstairs landing. 'Are you going anywhere in particular, Tam?'

She shook her head, not trusting herself to speak.

'Look, I know how you must be feeling. It's come as a shock to me, too. I'd be interested to know if Vicki's had any idea of what my parents are planning to do.'

Perhaps this was the real reason why Vicki had been so on edge recently, Tamsin thought. 'At least Vicki isn't facing the prospect of being homeless and having no job. It's a pity Fraser Kershaw's going to be renting that flat above The Chocolate House or we could have moved in there.'

Charlie's face was a picture. 'When did all this happen? You didn't tell me.'

'I thought you would have known, that's why, and with all that's been going on this week, we've been like ships that pass in the night.'

'True — look, as I've told Mum and Dad, Marissa and I are going for a drink. Why don't you join us?'

She shook her head. 'You'll have things to discuss. I don't suppose you'll be keeping this particular piece of information to yourself.'

'Absolutely not, although I'll have to warn Marissa to pretend to be surprised when Mum gets round to telling her. Come on, Tam. We're not likely to be by ourselves in the pub on a Saturday night, are we? There's karaoke.'

Tamsin forced a smile. 'How could I refuse? Okay — give me ten minutes.'

She didn't see Charlie grin and reach for his mobile as she went off to change. They picked up Marissa en route and, when they arrived, discovered Rob sitting in a corner nursing a drink.

'Oh good, you said you might be in here tonight,' Charlie greeted him and Tamsin wondered if it had been pre-arranged for her benefit. Oh, well, she could do with some cheerful company.

She shot Charlie a warning glance, hoping that he wouldn't discuss their family affairs in front of Rob. After all, it was possible that Vicki hadn't been told yet, and then — as Aunt Cathy had said — if their regular customers got wind of a rumour that Lambourne Caterers might be winding up, what little trade they'd got might evaporate.

After they'd been sitting for about an hour listening to the karaoke, and trying to make themselves heard above the din around them, Tamsin was beginning to get a headache. Glancing at her, Rob asked, 'Are you OK, Tam?'

'It is rather hot in here. I think I could do with some fresh air.'

'Good idea,' Charlie said. 'We could always find somewhere a bit quieter.'

Marissa looked disappointed. 'On a Saturday night — you must be kidding! Anyway, I'm beginning to enjoy myself. This is fun!'

'Tell you what,' Rob said, 'why don't

you two stay put, and Tamsin and I will go for a stroll by the river?'

When they got outside, Rob took Tamsin's arm. 'There's a nice Italian restaurant I know overlooking the river. Actually, I know the proprietor because when I was a student, I used to work there during the vacs. We can get cappuccinos there and have a quiet chat.'

It was cool strolling by the river and Tamsin began to relax. The lights twinkled like stars on the moored boats, and she could hear the gentle lapping of the water.

The restaurant was a pleasant venue which Tamsin hadn't visited before, but it was also quite crowded. The proprietor, Luigi, insisted on giving them cappuccinos and pastries on the house. They sat in an alcove which overlooked the river. It would, no doubt, be idyllic in the daytime.

For a moment, Tamsin was tempted to confide in Rob about what was going on in her family; but she was glad she didn't, because for the next half hour or so, he bent her ear about his work at the care home and his ideas for the future, and showed very little interest in her life.

When Rob began to tell Tamsin about Zoe, she decided that she'd had enough for one evening. He might pretend he'd got over Zoe, but Tamsin wasn't convinced. She told him she needed to freshen up, and made her way to the back of the restaurant.

'Hallo Tamsin, fancy seeing you here!' Fraser Kershaw was sitting at a table with Petrina Hornby, plus Lisa Clancy's brother, Warren, and his girlfriend.

'Fancy,' she said, forcing a smile.

'The food's good, isn't it?' Warren remarked. 'Are you weighing up the opposition?'

'No, actually Rob and I have just come in for a coffee.'

'Oh, is Rob here? Tell him to give me a bell sometime, will you, Tamsin?'

'Why don't you have a word with him

yourself — he's only over there.' She indicated their table and Rob raised a hand in greeting.

It wasn't until Tamsin was in the cloakroom a few minutes later that it occurred to her that she was hardly dressed for this sort of place. Fortunately, the lighting was rather dim, but she'd still been able to see that Fraser and Warren's companions had been wearing the latest fashions.

Obviously, Fraser didn't believe in wasting any time when it came to wining and dining Petrina Hornby. It was ridiculous, but Tamsin felt a little stab of jealousy and wished she hadn't seen them together.

'That was lucky, running into Warren Clancy like that,' Rob said when Tamsin returned to their table. 'I've been meaning to get in touch with him. We've just arranged to meet up for a round of golf — when we both have a window.'

'Golf! Since when have you played golf?' Tamsin asked in amazement.

Rob grinned. 'Oh, for a couple of years. It's a useful game to play. You'd be surprised at the amount of business that's carried out over a round of golf. Don't look at me like that, Tam! I could do with some networking.'

Tamsin wondered how he could afford it on a basic wage and, as if homing in on her thoughts, Rob said, 'My father will pay. He'll think it'll be a good investment to get me involved with my cousin's circle of friends!'

Tamsin, who had always believed in paying her own way, made no comment. She suddenly realised that she and Rob had grown poles apart; but she enjoyed his company and it was good to get out. There was no way she would have ventured into Luigi's for a coffee on her own.

Presently, as they walked back along the river to where Rob had parked his car he caught her hand in his. 'I've missed you, Tam. I hadn't realised how much until these past few weeks. So, now that your aunt and uncle are back, there's no reason why we shouldn't go out for that meal, is there? Perhaps in Luigi's?'

'Look, about that meal, Rob,' Tamsin said awkwardly. 'It's a really nice gesture, but why don't we go Dutch? Eating out is expensive.'

Immediately Tamsin had made the comment, she wished she could have retracted it. Rob let go her hand and stood stock-still on the path.

'Have you got the slightest idea how patronising that sounded, Tamsin?' he demanded coldly. 'I'm not exactly on the breadline, you know.'

'I'm sorry, Rob,' she said hastily, 'but, if you remember, years back we often split the bill.' She sighed. 'We're going to have to get to know each other all over again, aren't we?'

He visibly relaxed. 'I guess so. Perhaps we ought to start right now.' And, taking her in his arms, he gave her a gentle kiss which gradually became more impassioned. She could feel the heat of his body against hers; his hands moved slowly over her in a long, sensuous caress. She closed her eyes tightly, trying to recapture those enchanting, tender moments from years ago when they were both so very young and in love.

'So, how was that for starters?' he asked softly.

'Not bad, Mr Avery,' she said lightly, 'although I thought we'd agreed to keep our relationship strictly platonic.'

He released her reluctantly. 'That was just to remind you of the way things used to be between us.'

As Rob drove Tamsin home, she realised that she had been imagining that moment for so long. Deep down she had always hoped he'd come back to her, but the dreadful realisation was that she no longer had any feelings for him — other than those of a friend. His kiss had just proved that to her.

* * *

Cathy invited Vicki and her family to Sunday lunch so that she and Alec could tell them their news. Before they had the opportunity, however, Vicki came out with some of her own. They'd finished eating, and the children had got down from the table and were playing in a corner of the dining-room.

Bruce gave his wife a meaningful look. 'Vicki's got something she'd like to share with you,' he told everyone.

Vicki looked around the table and then announced with a little smile, 'I'm pregnant again, and this time it's twins!'

'Wow! How clever of you to double your family!' Tamsin told her, when she could get a word in edgeways.

It was a happy occasion, but after everyone had offered their congratulations, Alec and Cathy took their daughter and son-in-law into the sitting room for a quiet chat, whilst the others were clearing away.

When Alec had finished speaking, Vicki looked stunned. 'I'm pleased for you, truly I am,' she said at last. 'I know how you've often spoken of your dream of returning to Norfolk, Dad. It's just the suddenness of it all.'

She sniffed. 'I know I'm being utterly selfish, but I was really counting on your support. I'm going to need you both more than ever now. I honestly don't know how I'm going to manage. The thing is, Mum, I'm sick of the sight of chocolate. It makes me feel queasy, and I have to work with it every day *and* make all those cakes!'

Cathy put an arm round her daughter's shoulder. 'You're not to worry, love. I'm not planning to abandon you. We'll work through this — even if it means me staying on here for a while and your dad going on ahead to help Uncle Sam. Actually, I've just had a brilliant idea, although it would need thinking through. Listen, how would it be if . . . '

When she'd finished outlining her plan, everyone looked at her in admiration.

'That's a pretty good idea,' Alec told his wife. 'It would solve more than one problem. What do you two think?'

Bruce turned to Vicki. 'I think your mother's just come up with the perfect solution to a difficult situation. What d'you reckon?'

Vicki nodded. 'It's a very generous offer, but do you think Tamsin will agree?'

'Leave it to me,' her mother told her. 'It's just a pity your mother-in-law doesn't live a bit nearer. I'm sure she'd help out.'

Vicki shot her mother a horrified look, and Cathy had to smile as she thought of Betty Miles, who was likely to be more hindrance than help. She was a well-meaning lady, rather older than herself, who was more interested in how the children were dressed than in doing a turn with the washing and ironing.

'Now, you go in the garden and put your feet up, love, and I'll put the kettle on and make us all a nice cup of tea,' Cathy told her daughter.

'That sounds good; but before I do, there is one more thing we need to tell you both. Fraser Kershaw is moving into the flat above The Chocolate House.'

'Well, that *is* good news,' Alec said cheerfully. That's one less thing to worry about.'

★ ★ ★

Tamsin was taken aback when Cathy outlined her plan. 'You want me to help Vicki in The Chocolate House? But surely, if she's had to let the Saturday guy go, and is considering reducing Kelly's hours, she won't be able to pay my wages?'

'Don't worry about that, dear,' her aunt told her. 'If you agree, we're just going to loan you out. After all, we'd have been paying your wages here *and* we don't have to pay Harvey, so we'll get round it that way — for the time being, at least. Vicki's looking worn out, so it'll be a relief off my mind to know she's got some reliable help.'

'Absolutely! I'll do whatever I can to

help,' Tamsin assured her.

Aunt Cathy looked pleased. 'Thank you, dear. I thought you'd say that. I'm going to take over some of the baking, now that Pauline's helping me in the catering business. I have to say, I've been pleasantly surprised with her culinary skills this week. She's come up trumps. It was a good move on your part to employ her, Tamsin.'

'Actually, it was Marissa who suggested her mum might be able to help. We were in a tight spot so I took a chance.'

Aunt Cathy pushed back her dark hair. 'And it's paid dividends already. Well done! Bruce is going to take Vicki away for a holiday soon. He's found something on the internet — and we're going to have the children to stay with us. That way they can keep to their routine and continue going to nursery.'

Tamsin nodded. 'That's important. Have you got many functions lined up for next week?'

Cathy began measuring the ingredients for a cake. 'Three, but I've had a word with Angie and Pauline, and they think they can cope with the ones in the daytime — so that only leaves the Averys' dinner party, and we'll all need to lend a hand for that.'

Tamsin handed her the sieve. 'So, what had you got in mind for me to do?' she prompted.

'Well, if you can shadow Vicki for a couple of days — just to get the hang of things — although Kelly knows the ropes, of course. Can you pass me that bowl, dear?'

'There is just one thing bothering me,' Tamsin told her, passing her the bowl. 'Whilst I'm doing Vicki's job, who's going to be doing mine?'

'Oh, don't worry, I've thought of that too, Tam,' her aunt reassured her. 'Your uncle will man the office and check the post, and the accounts can be done as and when you can fit them in.'

There was little Tamsin could say to

this. She would just have to do the best she could to help out in a difficult situation.

She spent a hectic couple of days shadowing Vicki at the coffee shop. Kelly, who Tamsin had previously thought to be a congenial, friendly sort of girl, had scarcely two words to say to her. When they were left alone whilst Vicki made some necessary phone calls, Tamsin soon discovered what the problem was.

'Funny thing, you being here,' Kelly began. 'No sooner does Vicki tell me she's going to have to cut back my hours than you turn up.'

'But I'm only covering whilst Bruce and Vicki go on holiday. Surely she explained that?'

Kelly looked sulky. 'So why can't they leave me in charge? I'm perfectly capable of looking after things.'

'I'm sure you are,' Tamsin said soothingly, 'but it isn't a good idea for you to be left on your own, is it? I mean, every time you needed to go out the back you'd have to put the closed sign up, wouldn't you? And you're very vulnerable with the till and everything.'

'I suppose — anyway, I'm used to being in here on my own when Bruce or Vicki are out the back, so don't feel you've got to be around for me all of the time.'

*   *   *

'Oh dear, Kelly's changed since I've told her we're going to have to cut back her hours on a temporary basis,' Vicki said when Tamsin told her about the exchange of words.

'Oh, I expect she's just peeved because she was looking for more responsibility, not less,' Tamsin said, making light of it.

'Hmm, perhaps you're right. Anyway, we've told her it's just until business starts picking up again. Now, d'you suppose you could be an angel and keep an eye on things whilst I pick the children up from nursery? I need to have a word with their teachers about them staying with their grandparents whilst we're on holiday, and Bruce has gone to see his accountant.'

7

Vicki and Bruce's two small children, Jamie and Lucy, were adorable but demanding. Once they'd moved into their grandparents' house, everyone lent a hand and tried to keep them in their routine. The house became kiddy-orientated within twenty-four hours. Tamsin wondered how her cousin managed to maintain such an immaculate home.

Aunt Cathy had always been good at delegating. 'Tamsin, can you drop them off at the nursery this morning?' she asked on Monday morning. 'I'm tied up here. Now, make sure you tell Mrs Johnson that they'll be picked up at two o'clock by their grandfather.'

Tamsin arrived at The Chocolate House to find the door unlocked and Kelly already behind the counter. Seeing Tamsin's puzzled glance, she indicated the door leading to the stairs, which was also wide open. Before she could say anything, however, Fraser appeared.

'Good morning, Tamsin. I ought to have remembered punctuality isn't your strongest point. Good job I had a key or this young lady would still be standing outside.'

Tamsin, who had had a trying time searching in the lost property box for a missing indoor shoe belonging to Jamie, bristled at this remark. 'Having a key to the flat shouldn't mean you have to come in through the café,' she pointed out icily.

His blue eyes flashed with amusement. 'Absolutely,' he said reasonably, 'but, if you remember, the back yard is virtually inaccessible at present. Your cousins have suggested I come in the front way until we can get it sorted.'

Seeing the smirk on Kelly's face, Tamsin followed Fraser into the tiny passageway at the back of the shop and closed the door.

'Well, this is cosy,' Fraser remarked.

'Don't be ridiculous! Now, let's get one thing straight. I'm in charge of The Chocolate House whilst Vicki and Bruce are away, and I will not have you undermining my authority in front of Kelly. She's very impressionable.'

He caught her hands between his, sending a little frisson shuddering along her spine. 'Then we'd better not give her any food for thought.'

They both realised what he'd said, and laughed together at his unwitting joke. The moment of tension eased, but her close proximity to this man had set her pulse racing inexplicably. She could smell his tangy cologne; feel the warmth emanating from his body.

'What is it about you and confined spaces?' he asked, eyes twinkling.

She felt the colour suffuse her cheeks and, edging past him, pushed open the door. Fortunately, Kelly was occupied with serving an early customer.

'Lovely fellow, isn't he?' Kelly said presently when Tamsin emerged from the kitchen with some chocolate croissants.

'Who?' she asked innocently.

'The one who let me in. Don't remember his name. I was only introduced in passing by Bruce the other day.'

'Fraser Kershaw. He's Mrs Kershaw's son from Lavender Lodge. Do you know Mrs Kershaw?'

Kelly screwed up her face thoughtfully. 'I think I might have met her — very smart lady with short brown hair. She came in here the other day with some friends, now I come to think of it . . . What's happening about the chocolate cake? We've had at least two customers asking already.'

'My aunt's baking, even as we speak, but there won't be any until lunch-time — just the lemon, I'm afraid.'

'Our regular customers come in expecting the same things to be available,' Kelly commented with a toss of her head.

'Well, I think they might be in for a

pleasant surprise over the next couple of weeks because my aunt is experimenting with one or two different recipes,' Tamsin told her, as she gathered up some empty mugs.

Kelly paused in her task of replenishing the sugar bowls. 'They won't like it, you can take my word for it. Creatures of habit, that's what Vicki calls her regulars.'

Aunt Cathy called in presently with three scrumptious-looking gâteaux. 'Sorry, I got delayed, but the phone has never stopped ringing.'

'I thought Uncle Alec was dealing with the phone calls.'

'So he was, dear, but he had an appointment with the bank this morning, and he needs to get down to the allotment to pick up some veg for the dinner party at the Averys' tomorrow.' Aunt Cathy popped on a tabard. 'So, what needs doing here?'

'We're fairly well-organised so Kelly's gone for an early lunch break,' Tamsin told her. 'I've got the soup on and I'm making up the baguettes to order. We've had one or two customers with chocolate cake withdrawal symptoms.'

'Well, hopefully, from now on we can persuade them that the courgette and lime or almond and vanilla are equally as nice.'

'Sounds tempting to me,' came a voice from behind them.

Startled, Cathy swung round. Her face lit up. 'Fraser Kershaw! My goodness — you're so like your father! It must be years since I last saw you, but there's no mistaking who you are!'

Fraser grinned and took her outstretched hand. 'Cathy Lambourne! You haven't changed a bit.' And, reaching forward, he kissed her on the cheek.

Up until that moment, it hadn't occurred to Tamsin that Aunt Cathy had known Fraser when he was a boy.

'I've spent the morning humping and sorting boxes in the flat — with Bruce and Vicki's permission, obviously. It's dusty work and I'm feeling hungry, so I thought I'd throw myself on your mercy. The smell of that soup is tantalising.'

Cathy beamed. 'Sit yourself down and I'll get you some.'

He hesitated. 'I'm afraid I'm not exactly dressed for eating in here.'

Tamsin took in the elderly jeans and dark T-shirt, so different from his formal attire. Even his hair was tousled. She'd never seen him looking so casual and realised she liked it.

'Nonsense,' Cathy told him briskly. 'There's a table tucked away over there where no-one would notice if you were wearing a dustbin bag, but you look perfectly respectable to me. Tamsin, if you could carry on serving out here, I'll see to the baguettes.'

Tamsin ladled vegetable soup into a bowl, and placed that and some crusty bread on a tray. Apart from Fraser and three elderly ladies, The Chocolate House was empty. Hopefully, word hadn't got around about the lack of chocolate cake!

'Come and join me,' Fraser invited as

Tamsin placed his food in front of him.

'Well, I . . . ' She hesitated and, as if realising why, he called out to Cathy,

'I hate eating on my own, Mrs Lambourne, so perhaps Tamsin can have a coffee with me?'

'Yes, of course. We're pretty quiet at the moment.'

Tamsin served the elderly ladies before collecting the baguette her aunt had thoughtfully prepared for her.

'Be careful what you say, dear,' her aunt warned in a whisper, giving her a meaningful look. 'Best not to mention Norfolk or Vicki's condition for the present.'

Tamsin nodded and went to join Fraser.

'This soup is delicious,' he remarked.

'Vicki left it ready. So how are you getting on with the flat?'

'Slowly, there's a lot to shift. Bruce helped me with some of the boxes at the end of last week. This building fascinates me. To think there's been a café here all these years.'

'Yes, it's amazing, isn't it? And it's been in our family for generations. My great-grandparents lived here, and my grandparents. My Aunt Cathy and my father were both brought up here. Bruce and Vicki came to live in the flat too, when they first got married.'

Fraser broke off a piece of bread. 'Yes, and I realise that — until recent years — The Chocolate House was a tea shop. And, as you've told me, at one time the left-hand side of the building was a draper's. I'm glad I unearthed those postcards.'

'Yes, I haven't had an opportunity to show them to Aunt Cathy yet. I know she'll be interested. When Grandpa Jim retired he left a couple of elderly sisters to manage The Old Tea Shop. And then, when they too retired, the business premises stood empty for a time until Bruce and Vicki turned it into The Chocolate House.'

Fraser nodded, realising he was going to need to choose his words carefully to avoid putting his foot in it. He hoped

Cathy Lambourne would soon bring Tamsin up to speed with all that was going on.

He set down his spoon. 'I enjoyed that. So, what are you grinning at? Have I got soup round my mouth or what?'

'No — sorry! It's just that you seem to have developed a grey patch on your hair.'

'Where? Oh, that must have been when I was grovelling around in the attic. No wonder your aunt thought I looked like my father! She must have seen his photograph at Lavender Lodge.' He rubbed his hair with his handkerchief.

Catching the sound of their laughter, Cathy glanced in their direction. It was good to see them getting on so well. She just hoped things wouldn't change when her niece learnt what had happened regarding The Chocolate House.

Kelly rushed in, looking windswept. 'Sorry, Mrs Lambourne. There was a long queue in the supermarket. So what d'you want me to do?'

'A couple of coffees would be nice,' Fraser called out. 'Oh, and two portions of that very nice-looking gâteau — the almond and vanilla — if that's OK with you, Tamsin?'

'Fine — it's my favourite,' Tamsin smilingly assured him.

After a moment or two, Kelly called out, 'Coffee machine's on the blink again, Mr Kershaw.'

Fraser sprang to his feet and went to examine the machine.

'Bruce gives it a wham,' Kelly said helpfully.

Fraser obliged. 'Ah, yes, I see. There's nothing much wrong — the beans were sticking together!'

Tamsin grinned. 'I can see you're going to be an asset round here.'

Shortly afterwards the door opened again and Alec Lambourne appeared with Jamie and Lucy. He looked apologetically at his wife. 'I know you said to go straight home, but things took longer than expected this morning, so I haven't actually been to the allotment yet. As it's beginning to rain, I thought I'd better bring the children in here.'

'Oh, well, it can't be helped. But I really need those vegetables ASAP.'

'Perhaps they could have an ice-cream,' Alec suggested brightly.

'Ice-cream! Ice-cream!' chanted the children in unison.

'Now you've done it!' Cathy said. 'All right, you two — perhaps Tamsin can take you in the back, although there isn't much room.'

The café was beginning to fill up. 'Come and sit here,' Fraser offered.

Tamsin sorted out the children. Fraser looked amused as she popped a handful of paper napkins round each small neck and handed them a spoon. She took the bowls of ice-cream from her aunt.

'What's your name?' Fraser asked.

'Lucy, and he's Jamie. What's your name?' demanded the small blonde girl.

167

'Fraser . . . how old are you, Lucy?'

'Free, nearly four — how old are you, Fwaser?'

'Very old,' Fraser said without batting an eyelid. 'I'm thirty-three.'

Lucy was not impressed. 'My gwand-dad's older'n you. He's . . . '

'Lucy, that's enough,' admonished Tamsin.

The little girl dipped her spoon into her ice-cream. Jamie looked up and said, 'Joos peas.' He then managed to drop a large dollop of ice-cream on the tablecloth.

'Oh, dear, I'm so sorry,' Tamsin murmured and grabbed some kitchen roll from the counter.

Fraser laughed. 'Don't be. I can assure you I haven't had such an entertaining lunch-time for ages.' He picked up a couple of paper napkins and folded them deftly into animal shapes. The children were entranced and Tamsin found herself thinking what a good father he'd make.

'Tamsin, if you can take over here for

a bit, I'll run them home,' Aunt Cathy said. 'Who would have thought that two small children with two small bowls of ice-cream could have created such a mess?'

Fraser got to his feet, eyes twinkling. 'How much do I owe you, Mrs Lambourne?'

'Goodness, I should think it's us who owe you. It's on the house this time. Think of it as an early welcome present.'

'OK, thank you. I'm sure we'll be seeing more of each other over the next couple of weeks.'

* * *

Tamsin left The Chocolate House early in order to run one or two errands for Aunt Cathy. She was just coming out of the post office when she encountered Rob.

'You must be a mind-reader, Tam. I was just thinking about you,' he greeted her. 'Any chance of a chat?'

He didn't look his usual cheery self, and Tamsin wondered what was wrong. They walked through the nearby gardens and sat on a bench overlooking the river. It was a peaceful spot sheltered by willow trees.

'OK, Rob, what's wrong? Tell Aunty Tam all about it.'

'I didn't realise there was an empty flat above The Chocolate House until the other day. Neither you nor Charlie mentioned it when I said I was looking for a place of my own,' he burst out.

'For the very good reason it was still being used as storage space. Don't tell me you were interested in it, too?'

'I only learnt about it the other day from Warren. Trust Fraser to get in first! I couldn't believe it! Not content with Lavender Lodge, he's had to get his hands on The Chocolate House as well.'

'Hardly, Fraser's only renting the upstairs flat.' She saw Rob's surprised expression. 'What?'

'You obviously don't know, do you?'

he asked incredulously.

'Know what? Come on, Rob, you're not making much sense.'

But, Rob suddenly realised he'd already said too much and shook his head. 'I think you ought to have a word with your aunt and uncle. Let them fill you in. It's not up to me to say. It's a family matter.'

'Right, I'll do just that,' Tamsin assured him, feeling more mystified than ever, 'but, I have to say, I haven't got a clue as to what you're talking about.'

⋆ ⋆ ⋆

Tamsin didn't get the opportunity to speak with her aunt and uncle that evening, however, because they'd invited friends round to supper.

The following morning breakfast was a rushed affair. 'I just don't know how Vicki does it,' Aunt Cathy said. 'She certainly needs this holiday.'

'It seemed rather quiet at The

Chocolate House yesterday,' Tamsin remarked.

'Oh, but it was only Monday, Tamsin. You wait until it's market day. I'm sure we'll all be rushed off our feet then.'

'At least Fraser Kershaw's taken over the flat, so that'll be a bit more revenue coming in,' Charlie commented, reaching for another slice of toast. 'I mean, they're hardly going to let him live there rent-free, are they, now?'

Cathy exchanged a meaningful glance with her husband. 'There won't be any rent for the very simple reason that I'm afraid Bruce and Vicki don't own the property.'

There was a silence whilst Tamsin and Charlie assimilated this information.

'But we'd assumed Grandpa Jim owned the entire property, and so when he died . . . ' Tamsin began.

'Yes, dear,' her aunt said gently. 'He certainly did own it at one time, but things changed.'

Charlie tried to get his head round this. 'But I'd understood it had been in the family for generations. Grandpa Jim was brought up there, and he and Grandma Lacey lived above the tea-rooms for most of their married lives, didn't they? And you and Tamsin's father were brought up there, too, weren't you, Mum?'

His mother looked sad. 'Yes, we were, but it's not as simple as that, Charlie.'

'So that's what Rob Avery was hinting at yesterday. OK, so if Grandpa Jim didn't own it, then who did — still does, I suppose?' asked Tamsin impatiently. 'Gerald and Drusilla Clancy, perhaps?'

Her uncle Alec shook his head. 'Not the Clancys, no.'

'I think you've said enough for now, Alec. After all, it's Vicki and Bruce's affair, and they're not here to explain things,' Cathy pointed out.

But Alec wasn't to be put off. 'If it hadn't been for The Chocolate House, I don't think we'd have learnt about this until after your grandfather died. Apparently, he thought we'd be upset, as indeed we were.'

Charlie stared at his parents blankly, and it was left to Tamsin to ask once again, 'So who did he sell it to?'

Cathy and Alec exchanged glances again, and then Alec cleared his throat and said, 'He sold it to Georgina Kershaw.'

'Mrs Kershaw owns Grandpa Jim's place!' exclaimed Tamsin. 'But why? I mean, why would she have wanted to buy it from him and then leave the flat standing empty?'

Aunt Cathy sighed. 'It's complicated, my dears, and I really haven't got the time to go into it all now or the children will be late for nursery.'

'So, let's get this straight. Fraser is renting the flat, courtesy of his mother,' Charlie said slowly.

'If only it were that simple,' put in Alec. 'We might as well tell them, Cathy.'

Cathy nodded resignedly. 'Mrs Kershaw doesn't own the property any more. It seems she didn't buy it for herself.'

Charlie and Tamsin's attention was riveted on Cathy Lambourne. 'So, if she doesn't own it — then who on earth does?' asked Charlie.

'She, er, bought it as a gift for her son,' Alec finished for his wife, after a long pause. 'The entire property now belongs to Fraser Kershaw.'

'Fraser Kershaw!' Tamsin echoed. 'You're saying that he owns The Chocolate House?'

'Well, no, not exactly. As your uncle's just told you, he owns the property, which includes the business premises.'

★   ★   ★

Rob Avery called into the coffee shop just before lunch-time, on his way to work. 'I know it's a bit last-minute, Tam, but would you like to come to our dinner party tonight?'

175

Tamsin finished serving a customer before turning back to him. 'Sorry, Rob; actually, I'm already coming to your dinner-party tonight, but I'll be helping Aunt Cathy with the catering. Even if I weren't, I couldn't very well let the other members of the team wait on me, could I now? Why? Has someone dropped out?'

Rob looked awkward. 'No, nothing like that. It's a genuine invitation. I thought I was working but I've had to change shifts with someone, that's all, so Mum thought it would be nice for me to invite a friend.'

He pulled up a stool and drank his cappuccino at the counter. 'Guess who they'll ask to make the numbers up now?'

Tamsin shook her head.

'Alison — Dad's practice nurse. Apparently, she's rather keen on me.'

Tamsin thought of Alison, a chirpy, attractive blonde girl. 'Isn't she, er, just a bit young for you?'

He nodded. 'Probably, but I can't

help it if my charm is such that all these young ladies keep falling over themselves to be with me, can I now?'

'No, but you can help being on such a big ego trip,' she told him sternly. 'If you're not careful, it'll be you that ends up falling over! Now, if you don't mind, it's getting busy in here. I'll see you this evening.'

He grinned and got to his feet. Reaching over the counter he placed his hand over hers and, lowering his voice, asked, 'How about coming to Luigi's with me one evening next week?'

'I'll check the roster and let you know.'

'Luigi asked me where the pretty lady was, the last time I called in; and before you ask, no, it's not a freebie, but he has said he'll let me have whatever we choose for a special price.'

'The thought hadn't even crossed my mind, Rob. I'd like to come but I'm not sure if I can get away at the moment. We're looking after Vicki's youngsters whilst she and Bruce are on holiday, and someone's got to be around to babysit in the evenings because Aunt Cathy's very often tied up.'

Rob looked downcast. 'That's two invitations you've turned down in a matter of minutes. I was hoping we could have a nice quiet meal away from our families; although come to think of it, even Luigi's was frequented by my cousins . . . Have you had a chance to ask your folks about that little matter we discussed yesterday?'

She nodded and, aware of Kelly's curious eyes on her, walked with Rob to the door and followed him outside.

'I'm as stunned as you are — still trying to get my head round it . . . Look, we'll have to talk later. This is neither the time nor the place.'

'If it wasn't for my mother's dinner party this evening, I'd have it out with Fraser,' he said bitterly. 'My Uncle Gerald has worked his socks off at the chocolate factory all these years, whilst Gil Kershaw swanned off to do his own thing.'

'If anyone ought to be miffed with Fraser, it's me,' she told him. 'After all, this place has been in my family for generations, and now suddenly I've discovered it belongs to Fraser.'

'Right, if you want to speak to him about it — now's your opportunity. Here he comes. I'll leave you to it,' Rob said, a glint in his eyes as he walked smartly away.

'Speak to me about what?' Fraser asked, opening the door for her.

'It'll keep,' she told him shortly. 'After all, you weren't in any hurry to explain things to me, were you? You just let me go prattling on about how The Chocolate House has been in my family for generations, instead of being straight with me. If it hadn't been for Rob . . . '

His eyes narrowed. 'Ah, yes, Rob; I might have guessed. I'm sorry you've had to find out like this, Tamsin, but I was specifically asked not to say anything for the time being. Look, I'll be in the flat until around three o'clock.

Why not come and have lunch with me today, and we'll have a chat about things.'

They'd reached the counter, and he had to wait for a reply until she'd served a couple of elderly customers with hot chocolate and popped their teacakes under the grill.

'OK,' she said. 'I've certainly got no intention of discussing my family affairs in public. Anyway, my aunt and uncle have told me a certain amount already.'

'Good . . . Actually, I wouldn't mind a coffee right now,' he told her. He moved her gently aside so that he could stand beside her behind the counter. Her heart began to pound at his closeness.

'Attend to your customers. I'll serve myself and leave the money just here — watch out! The teacakes are burning!' The warning came too late. 'Don't worry, I'll have them. I like burnt offerings — even if they are supposed to be bad for you. I'll have a chicken mayo baguette and some lemon cake for lunch. Oh, and more coffee, please. Choose what you like for yourself — my treat.'

He was incorrigible. Presently, he marched off upstairs with a tray bearing the coffee and teacakes. 'See you later,' he called back over his shoulder.

'What was all that about?' Kelly asked curiously.

'Oh, nothing to worry about,' Tamsin told her, wishing it were true. She wondered if her mother knew that The Chocolate House premises no longer belonged to the family. There were a number of questions Tamsin still needed to ask Aunt Cathy. It had all come as a bolt from the blue. And what on earth was the problem between Fraser and Rob?

For the next hour Tamsin didn't have a moment to breathe. Trade seemed to have picked up, probably due to a sudden sharp downpour of rain that drove people to seek shelter. Kelly was despatched to attend to the shop, which had been rather neglected over the past few days, and Cathy couldn't help out that morning as she was up to her eyes in preparation for that evening's dinner party.

Fortunately, Uncle Alec had said he'd drop by for an hour or so before picking up the children from nursery. Just as Tamsin was wondering where he'd got to the phone rang.

'Your uncle's had to fetch Jamie from nursery,' came Aunt Cathy's voice. 'He's had a bit of a tumble and he's feeling a bit sorry for himself. Alec's had him checked over by Dr Avery. It's nothing serious, but he's missing his mummy, so we've decided to keep him at home for the rest of the day.

'Now, can you manage on your own while Kelly goes to lunch? To be honest, I'm up to my eyes here. Angie's coming in to help for an hour or so presently, but Pauline's occupied until later on.'

'Of course I can. Not to worry, just so long as Jamie's all right,' Tamsin assured her.

Charlie and Marissa put in an appearance just before Kelly was due to go off duty. Tamsin raised her eyebrows. 'Let me guess — Aunt Cathy's asked you to drop in?'

'Ten out of ten,' Charlie grinned. 'She's offered to pay for our lunch if we cover for you for half an hour or so. It was an offer we couldn't refuse.'

Tamsin served their lunch, thinking this was typical of Aunt Cathy. Aware that Kelly was watching her intently, Tamsin made a point of writing an IOU for her aunt and posting it in a prominent position behind the till. She couldn't help wondering if Kelly was making a mental note of any freebies Tamsin's family might be having. There was something about the girl's attitude that bothered her.

8

Presently, Tamsin collected some lunch for herself and Fraser and, climbing the stairs, knocked on the half-open sitting-room door.

'Come in,' called Fraser.

He was sitting on a plastic crate at a folding table, working on his laptop and looking very businesslike in spite of his casual attire. He removed his glasses.

'Ah, lunch. Good, I'm ravenous! Come and sit down, although I'm afraid I can only offer you a beanbag to sit on for the moment. It's a bit spartan in here.'

'I'm surprised you're working from here. It can't be very comfortable,' she said curiously, looking round the large room which was virtually empty, apart from a pile of boxes and oddments stacked against one wall.

'I've discovered that's the best sort of

environment to work in — few distractions and relatively quiet. My mother's got some sort of committee meeting at Lavender Lodge this morning. I could go into the factory but decided to stay here instead. Anyway, let's have lunch first, and then we can have that chat.'

'OK, but I haven't got too long. It's really busy downstairs today and Marissa and Charlie are covering for a short while.'

After they'd finished eating, Fraser stacked the empty plates on a tray. 'That was absolutely delicious. I'm impressed by the high standard of food served here . . . So, come on, Tamsin. What's bothering you?'

Tamsin, perched on a squashy red beanbag, felt at a disadvantage, so she got up and went to sit on the window seat instead. She came straight to the point.

'You've neglected to tell me you're about to become the new owner of this building,' she burst out.

Fraser studied his computer screen for a few minutes before turning back to her. 'Yes, I thought that was it, but why should it bother you so much?'

Tamsin gasped. 'What happens to my family is very much my concern. No wonder Vicki's been looking so stressed recently. The Chocolate House is their livelihood.'

Fraser frowned 'So what's the problem? Nothing's changed regarding the business unless ... Oh, I see, you're worrying about the rent I'm going to be charging them, aren't you?'

She nodded. 'That, amongst other things. I was aware that, although The Chocolate House was Vicki and Bruce's brainchild, they only managed it for my grandfather. It was their business in everything but name. Now, I understand why.'

Fraser nodded. 'It was simpler that way. When he sold the property to my mother, he naturally retained the lease on The Old Tea Shop. My mother and your grandfather came to an amicable arrangement about the rent. He only paid her a peppercorn sum for a considerable time; and since his death, whilst things are being sorted out, there's been nothing at all.'

Tamsin swallowed as his words hit home. 'I hadn't realised . . . I've never dealt with The Chocolate House accounts. I suppose it really is none of my business.'

He nodded. 'But I can understand why you're concerned for your family. I still have to discuss things in some detail with Vicki and Bruce, but in the meantime, I'd advise you not to let your imagination work overtime.'

Tamsin sprang from the sill and went to stand in front of him. 'That's all very well, Fraser, but it would have been better if you'd explained things to me from the outset. The Lambournes and the Miles have been very good to me.'

His eyes widened. 'I can assure you that whatever transpires, I'll be fair. However, I'm sure you'll agree that it wouldn't make good business sense for me to continue allowing Vicki and Bruce to have the premises free of charge, so I'm afraid that — just as soon as things are settled — they'll be asked to pay a realistic rent.'

'Up until recently, Charlie and I believed my grandfather still owned this property,' Tamsin said quietly. 'It's come as a bit of a shock to find he didn't.'

His expression softened. 'Yes, I'm sure it has, but your grandfather had his reasons for selling it. My mother has naturally explained everything to me, and I hope your aunt and uncle will, in turn, explain things to you. It would be better coming from them.'

Fraser doodled on a piece of paper in front of him and then, coming to a sudden decision, looked up. 'There's something else I ought to explain. My mother inherited quite a substantial amount of money from my father when he died. She saw buying this property as a way of making a good, long-term investment; and, of course, it solved your grandfather's immediate cash-flow problem.'

'But I'm not sure I understand why she'd want to buy this particular property,' Tamsin said curiously.

His blue eyes met hers in a searching look. 'You really don't know, do you?'

She shook her head.

'It's because she and my father lodged with your grandparents for a time when they first got married. Actually, I was born here.'

She stared at him in disbelief. This was the last thing she'd expected to hear. 'Are you sure?'

Fraser laughed. 'Well, I don't actually remember the occasion, if that's what you mean, but my mother ought to know. I was a bit premature and she was taken by surprise. I spent the first two years of my life here. So you see, in some ways, I've got more claim to it than you have.'

'I don't know how you make that out,' Tamsin said unsteadily. 'For me, this is a memory place. You see, when I was a child we moved around a lot — never settled anywhere for long — but my father used to visit his parents as often as he could, and he'd always bring me with him.

'Then, when he went to work abroad, his leave times were precious, but we still came here. I was only ten when he died — an accident on an oil rig. Mum and I stayed here for a few months and then we moved in with the Lambournes.'

Fraser got up from his perch on the crate and came to sit beside her on the floor.

'My mother isn't sentimental, Fraser. She got rid of most of his stuff, apart from a few photographs, but this place — this is where the memories are, and now that Grandpa Jim has died . . . Well, I thought it would belong to our family for ever!' She turned her head away, but not before he'd seen the tears in her eyes.

He patted her shoulder. 'Hey, I'm not planning to do anything too drastic to this building. You're welcome to come up here whenever you like.'

Tamsin scrabbled for her handkerchief. 'I don't know what's wrong with me. I'm not usually so emotional. I think it's suddenly hit me. Grandpa Jim only died three months ago, and . . . ' She swallowed. 'He was a very special person.'

Fraser flung a comforting arm about her shoulders and drew her close. 'Yes, I realise that from what my mother's told me. Anyway, I met him a few times over the years. My mother spent a fair amount of time chatting to him about the good old days. Oh, she knew your grandfather pretty well.'

'I just don't understand why he didn't tell us what he'd done.'

'Sometimes, Tamsin,' Fraser said gently, giving her a hug, 'it's better to present things as a *fait accompli*; that way there can be no arguments, no recriminations.'

He would have liked to have told her his side of the story, but was aware that

191

now wouldn't be a good time.

Tamsin had come to confront him about his deception in keeping his ownership of The Chocolate House to himself. Now, in the shelter of his arms, she felt her anger subside. She could feel the comforting warmth of his muscular body against hers, and her heartbeat quickened. She had a sudden overwhelming desire to reach out and touch him; to entwine her fingers in his thick hair.

'So, what else is worrying you?' he prompted, and she pulled herself together with an effort. She knew she couldn't tell him what was really at the back of her mind, which was: what would happen should he decide to turn the entire property back into a house? 'What is it between you and Rob Avery?' she asked instead.

Fraser looked startled. 'Oh, it dates back to a bit of sibling rivalry between my father and his stepbrother and sister. My Uncle Gerald and Aunt Susan felt that Lavender Lodge should have been left to the three of them, and not just to my father. And now that The Chocolate House has also slipped through their fingers . . . '

Tamsin nodded. 'I suppose Gerald Clancy thought it would be a good acquisition for his business.'

Fraser scrambled to his feet and dusted himself down. 'Oh, he'd have converted it into offices or whatever would have fetched the most revenue. So, you see, that's why my mother didn't admit to having bought the property from your grandfather.

'Once your grandfather had died, Gerald didn't waste any time in approaching your aunt and uncle to see if they would sell it to him, and he wasn't too happy to discover it belonged to my mother.'

Tamsin gasped. 'I'd no idea about any of this, Fraser.'

'Actually, there is a little more to the story, but I'll leave it to your aunt and uncle to fill you in . . . Now, unfortunately, I've got to attend a meeting at the factory shortly, and must have this presentation ready. I'll need to print it out when I get there.'

He held out his hands and pulled her to her feet. 'The sooner I can get my kitchen sorted out, the better; then I can offer you a cup of tea. So, where did you used to stay when you came here as a child?'

'Oh, right up on the top floor. There's a wonderful view from there — right over the town. I know I'm being sentimental and I'm not ashamed to admit it.'

'And why should you be?' he asked softly. 'It's good to have those kinds of memories.' He reached out and gently ran a finger down her cheek. 'It's a side of you I rather like, Tamsin Lacey.' And, bending forward, he brushed her mouth gently with his lips.

It was a butterfly kiss stirring her emotions and leaving her yearning for more. Their eyes met and held for a moment before he released her. She gave him a tremulous little smile, and then picking up the tray, went downstairs to the café with a light heart. She was glad that they'd sorted out their differences, because she knew she was physically attracted to this man.

* * *

As they were getting organised for the Averys' dinner party that evening, Tamsin mentioned the conversation she'd had with Fraser to Aunt Cathy.

'Oh, so he's told you then! Yes, Tamsin, it's true, but it was a long time ago and I don't suppose Mrs Kershaw wants to be reminded of it. A lot of water has flowed under the bridge since then, and her circumstances have greatly changed . . . Now, I've prepared some supper for us. I can't have you going all evening on an empty stomach.

'The dinner party's not till eight o'clock because of Dr Avery's evening surgery, and I'm quite organised. Susan Avery's seeing to the table herself . . .

Whilst we're eating, I'll tell you the rest of the story. It's a pity Charlie isn't back yet, but Alec will fill him in when they have their meal later on. He's getting the children ready for bed just now.'

Tamsin never ceased to marvel at her aunt's efficiency. She supposed it was where Vicki got it from.

Presently, as Tamsin tucked into the appetising casserole, Cathy said, 'You know that your Grandpa Jim was always such a generous man? He gave away more than he kept. Over the years, he put money into Lambourne Caterers and helped the three of you when you were getting your qualifications. We've also all benefitted from the legacies he's left us. Well, he wanted to help Vicki and Bruce get on the property ladder, so he gave them some money for a deposit — as I expect you're aware.'

Tamsin nodded, wondering what was coming next.

Her aunt helped herself to vegetables. 'In doing all of this, he had to raise some capital, so — completely unbe-known to us at the time — he took out a substantial loan; and before you ask, no, not from the bank or Georgina Kershaw.'

'Then who?' asked Tamsin curiously.

'Gerald Clancy. He's an astute businessman and believed that, ulti-mately, your grandfather would sell him the property.'

Tamsin frowned. 'So I suppose Grandpa Jim couldn't pay back the loan?'

'That's it in a nutshell! Gerald was greedy. He raised the interest rate annually so that your grandfather had a struggle to make ends meet.'

Cathy sighed. 'So, in the end, he sold the property to Mrs Kershaw, and paid back the loan without breathing a word about what he'd done. Both he and Georgina Kershaw kept the change of ownership a secret.'

Tamsin was struggling to understand. 'But how did Mrs K come to know about Grandpa Jim's predicament?'

'Well, they confided in one another, you see. Your grandparents and the Kershaws go back a long way, and they've always kept in touch. Anyway, although he sold the property to Georgina, he arranged to retain a lease for the business premises, because at that time the Holmes sisters were still managing the tea shop on his behalf. He also paid the rent on the flat, as Vicki and Bruce were still living there then.'

Cathy concentrated on her meal for a few moments, and then added, 'All this only came to light when Vicki and Bruce asked if they could rent The Old Tea Shop premises off your grandfather when the sisters retired. Well, as you can imagine, he hadn't expected that, but he was able to put a substantial amount into the new business. Otherwise, as I've said before, I don't think we'd have learnt about this until after your grandfather died.'

Aunt Cathy shot to her feet and gathered up the empty plates. 'Now, any more questions will have to wait. We'd best get ready. The time's marching on.'

* * *

When they arrived at the Averys' elegant, detached house, Tamsin could have wished she'd have stayed at home, because the first person she set eyes on was Fraser: sitting on the terrace with his mother and Petrina Hornby — who was looking like a fashion model, wearing a designer dress.

'What a beautiful evening it is,' Georgina called out to them. 'It seems an age since we met up for a chat, Cathy. Did you enjoy your holiday?'

'It was wonderful,' Cathy told her. 'But we're extra busy at present, because Vicki and Bruce are away, and so we're looking after both The Chocolate House and the children.'

'So Fraser tells me. Sounds like a bit of a juggling act to me. I just don't know how you manage it.'

Fraser's expression was bland, and Tamsin wondered if he'd relayed their conversation from earlier in the day to his mother. The few moments of intimacy in his flat now had a dream-like quality. How could she have imagined it had meant anything to him? Beside Petrina Hornby, she must seem like a gauche adolescent. Thankfully, she followed her aunt into the house.

Susan Avery came into the kitchen looking flustered. 'I've done my best with the table, but if you could just cast an eye over it, Tamsin — just to make sure I've remembered everything.'

Tamsin accompanied Mrs Avery into the dining-room and studied the beautifully-laid table with its dazzling white linen, gleaming cutlery and sparkling crystal glasses.

'That's fine, Mrs Avery — very nice. The only thing is — perhaps you should move the flowers. It's a beautiful arrangement, but rather large, and we don't want any accidents.'

Susan Avery followed Tamsin's advice and then said awkwardly, 'I'm sorry if Robert embarrassed you, my dear, by inviting you to be a guest tonight. I told him it wouldn't be appropriate for you as your aunt was the caterer, but he just wouldn't listen.'

'Yes, I explained that it would have been awkward,' Tamsin told her, trying not to feel indignant. In the past, the Averys had made it abundantly clear that Tamsin wasn't good enough for their son.

Susan Avery gave a tight little smile. 'Anyway, we've asked my husband's young practice nurse, Alison, along. Her father's a consultant at a London hospital and we're rather hoping she might introduce Robert to him. He could do with some contacts.'

Tamsin murmured something polite. Poor Rob, why wouldn't his parents just accept that he was happy enough doing the job he was doing? She was heartily relieved she could remain in the kitchen for most of that evening.

'Whoever is that blonde girl making sheep's eyes at Rob Avery?' asked Pauline Wise, coming into the kitchen with a tray of dirty dishes.

Tamsin cleared a space. 'Alison somebody — apparently she's a nurse at Dr Avery's practice.'

'Well, if my Marissa went out dressed like that, I'd have something to say about it,' Pauline pronounced.

Cathy raised her eyebrows but made no comment. She and her family had learnt that they had to be the soul of discretion at dinner parties, and never, ever repeat what they saw or heard if they wanted to remain in business.

★ ★ ★

'Well, that seemed to go very smoothly; Susan Avery seemed very pleased with everything,' Cathy said, as she and Tamsin were clearing away at the end of the evening after the guests had departed. Pauline had already left, taking Marissa and Angie with her. Suddenly, Georgina Kershaw popped her head round the kitchen door.

'Oh good, you are still here. Can I throw myself on your mercy?'

'Why, whatever's wrong?' asked Cathy, pausing in her task of gathering up the empty containers.

'Nothing disastrous, but there's a problem with the transport and Susan looks so tired. I think she must be aching for her bed. Fraser's doing a chauffeuring act because Gerald's car wouldn't start. James Avery was going to run me home, but he's been called out to one of his patients at the nursing home, and Rob's already left with Alison. So do you think I could cadge a lift in your van?'

'Yes, of course you can — Tamsin won't mind travelling in the back, will you, dear?'

Tamsin shook her head.

'Wonderful — I'll pop and tell Susan. Splendid meal as ever, Cathy!'

It was only a short drive to Lavender Lodge. Fraser's car was already on the drive, and Tamsin was just about to scramble out of the back of the van, when he appeared and reached up to help her down. Her heart lurched as his fingers made contact with hers.

'Come and have a nightcap,' Georgina invited. 'How about some hot chocolate?'

'Well, that would be very nice — just for a short while though,' Cathy told her, picking up her mobile to ring Alec.

Presently, they sat in the gracious sitting-room, enjoying mugs of chocolate with marshmallows floating on the top, and small savoury biscuits that melted in the mouth.

'Well, I got my ride in the van at last,' Georgina said, 'and I thoroughly enjoyed it.'

'You'd better ask Uncle Gerald if he's got a vacancy for a van driver,' Fraser joked and everyone laughed.

'Tamsin was surprised to learn I'd been born above The Old Tea Shop,'

Fraser remarked.

'Not half as surprised as I was,' his mother retorted drily. 'Were you shocked to hear that my son is taking up permanent residence at The Chocolate House, Tamsin?'

'Well, it was a bit unexpected, but I suppose I'll get used to it,' she said, smiling at Fraser.

'It seems a number of people have been a bit put out by the change of ownership,' Mrs Kershaw continued. 'Susan Avery was bending my ear about it just now. Apparently Rob had got his sights set on the flat for himself.'

Was that why Georgina had been so anxious to have a lift home? Tamsin wondered.

Fraser set down his mug. 'Well, someone had to be disappointed . . . Now, you might like to know that one of the first things I intend to do is to sort out the security. Just as soon as Vicki and Bruce return, I shall discuss the idea of metal window shutters with them. Top of my list is to get a secure internal door fitted at the top of the stairs, and another at the back leading to the yard.'

'That's a brilliant idea,' Cathy enthused. 'Anything to deter any more break-ins.' Catching sight of the time, she sprang to her feet. 'That was delicious and very welcome, but we'd best be making tracks or Alec will be sending out a search party.'

'Well, it was your mother who showed me how to make proper hot chocolate. She was such a lovely lady. Remind me to show you those post-cards some time, Cathy. They're a real find.'

'I'll be interested to see them — pity I missed the meeting.'

Fraser walked with them to the van. 'I'll see you at The Chocolate House tomorrow,' he told Tamsin. 'I'm really looking forward to moving in.'

And Tamsin realised that she was looking forward to it too.

* * *

It had been a strange sort of evening, Tamsin realised, as she got ready for bed. For a brief time there had been two men in her life, and it been an uncomfortable experience seeing them both with other women at the dinner party.

She found herself considering which of them she'd have chosen to partner her that evening — and knew that, without a shadow of doubt, it would have been Fraser. Remembering his kiss, she smiled and hugged the memory to her.

9

Tamsin realised she was enjoying working at The Chocolate House more than she would ever have believed possible. Kelly seemed a lot happier, which made for a pleasant atmosphere.

'Tyler's got himself a new job working in a supermarket on Saturdays,' she told Tamsin on Wednesday, as she refilled the stands of paper napkins at lunchtime.

'Tyler?' Tamsin queried.

'Yes, you know, the guy who worked here for a while. Saw him at the Leisure Centre last night.'

'Well, that's good news.' Tamsin paused to serve a customer.

'Mmm — says he never really liked working here anyway, but he wasn't well pleased when Vicki told him she couldn't afford to keep him on . . . Oh, hallo, Fraser.'

Tamsin's heart missed a beat as he came across to the counter.

'Hi . . . Tamsin, I completely forgot to tell you the electrician will be in tomorrow to check the wiring in the flat and put in some additional power points. And then, from next Tuesday, the decorators will be around for several days.'

'Right, so I suppose we can expect to have a stream of workmen parading through the shop,' Tamsin said, tongue-in-cheek, as she handed a lady her change.

'What? Oh, I hope not. I don't want to cause too much disruption,' Fraser told her. 'The sooner I can get the back yard cleared, the better.'

Tamsin grinned. 'Only joking — I realise you'll need to get things sorted out in the flat . . . Goodness, this place is like Piccadilly Circus this morning! Here's Charlie!'

Charlie was clutching a large cake box. 'One chocolate gâteau as promised. I had an SOS from Mum. She's rather tied up, Tamsin. Apparently, she'd completely forgotten she'd promised to take old Mrs Perkins shopping this afternoon.'

'No problem. We're managing just fine, aren't we, Kelly?'

Kelly nodded and Charlie set the cake on the counter. 'Right then, I'll just grab a quick bite to eat before heading back to work.'

'Great minds think alike — mind if I join you?' asked Fraser. He sat down opposite Charlie and they fell into an easy discussion about sport.

'My father was telling me about your connections with this place,' Charlie said presently, as he tucked into his baguette.

'Yes, it means a lot to my mother. I hope you don't think too badly of me for taking it over.'

Charlie shrugged. 'I'd rather it was you than the Clancys, although I'll admit it was a bit of a shock to discover it had been sold. My family kept that quiet. So what brought you back here?'

They were sitting near enough to the counter for Tamsin to overhear their conversation, and she thought Fraser seemed surprised by the question. She got the distinct impression that he would have preferred not to answer it, but he said pleasantly enough, 'Oh, I just felt like a change of scenery. The firm I worked for in Bristol was moving to London, and Stanfield seemed like a better option, so I accepted redundancy.'

When Charlie had left, Fraser cleared the table, and was just about to go upstairs when Rob came into the café. Ignoring Fraser he turned to Tamsin.

'Hi, Tam, I've been trying to get hold of you but you've not been answering my messages.'

'That's because I've left my mobile at home,' Tamsin told him. 'Is it urgent, Rob? We're quite busy, as you can see.'

Fraser consulted his watch. 'I'd offer to cover for you, Tamsin, but I'm due at work shortly.'

'Likewise,' Rob told him. Anyway,

this'll only take a minute. Are you free tomorrow evening, Tamsin? I'd like to take you out to dinner at Luigi's.'

'I — um,' Tamsin mumbled, uncomfortably aware of Fraser's intent gaze. The colour suffused her cheeks. Why on earth couldn't Rob have waited until his cousin had left the premises before inviting her out? Now Fraser would think she and Rob were back in a relationship.

'Good choice, I'd thoroughly recommend it,' Fraser remarked, as he gathered up his jacket and made for the door.

Just then, several customers came into the café and, whilst Tamsin took their orders, Rob propped his elbows on the counter and waited until she'd finished.

'There's something I'd like to talk to you about,' he said at length. 'So, d'you think you can make tomorrow evening?'

Tamsin deftly placed two scoops of chocolate ice-cream into a sundae dish, covered them with sprinkles and popped on a wafer before replying. 'Thanks, Rob, I'll look forward to that.'

He gave her a broad grin. 'Phew, I thought you were about to turn me down again. I'll text you regarding the time.' He helped himself to a chocolate from the dish of Clancy's samples on the counter before leaving the café.

'Wasn't that Dr Avery's son?' Kelly asked curiously, as she collected the tray of ice-cream. 'I didn't know you two were going out.'

'Oh, we're old friends — used to go to the same school,' Tamsin said lightly. She wondered what Rob had told Fraser about their past relationship. Probably enough to make him misinterpret the situation between them now.

Tamsin wished Rob had just left a message on the answerphone at home. She decided she'd go out to dinner with him the following evening as arranged, listen to what he had to tell her, and then let him know that she just wasn't interested in seeing him anymore. Deep down, she knew it was because she was becoming increasingly attracted to Fraser Kershaw.

★   ★   ★

On Thursday evening, Tamsin dressed for the occasion in a strappy pink dress she'd bought for a friend's wedding a couple of years back.

'Wow!' Rob said approvingly when he saw her. 'I'd forgotten what you looked like when you were dressed to kill, Tam.'

She laughed. 'I take it that was intended to be a compliment? You don't look so bad yourself, although not nearly so formal as you did the other evening.'

'Oh, well, you know my parents. They want everything to be just so and everyone to dress accordingly.'

'And did you have an enjoyable evening?' she asked rather wickedly.

'Yes, it was all right. Alison's a great girl, but not my type — if that's what you mean. As you said, she's a little young for me. Mind you, we had a very useful conversation and, thanks to her, I've got an idea of what I want to do with my life now.'

'But I thought you enjoyed working with the old people.'

He nodded. 'So I do. They're delightful and very interesting. It's rewarding work in its own way, but I'm not sure if it's my vocation.'

They arrived at Luigi's and, when he'd taken their order, they sat chatting in the attractive alcove overlooking the river. 'OK, so fire away. What's this idea you've got for your new career?' Tamsin asked curiously.

'I'm considering training as a nurse,' he said in a rush.

This was so unexpected that Tamsin remained silent for a few minutes.

'Rob, have you really thought this through?' she asked at length. 'I mean, it's an admirable profession, but there's a lot more fetching and carrying than if you were a doctor.'

He nodded. 'Not much different from now, then, except that — with the proper training — I'd have more options *and* earn more money. Anyway, I thought I'd run it by you — see what you thought.'

'Actually, I think it's an excellent idea, Rob,' she told him genuinely. 'And if you're really sure it's what you want to do, then go for it. I think it will require a lot of commitment, though.'

He nodded. 'I'm prepared to give it that.'

Just then their main course arrived and they tucked into the pasta with appreciation. It was delicious. Rob poured her a glass of wine. 'Of course, the biggest hurdle will be convincing my parents.'

'Robert Avery, you've got to learn to stand up to them. If you had, you'd have known where you were going from the outset.'

Rob shrugged as he twisted the spaghetti round his fork. 'Look who's talking! I seem to remember you gave up your job to come back here.'

'That was different. It was my decision. Anyway, I'm really pleased I did because I got to know Grandpa Jim so much better over those last few years, and now . . . ' She trailed off, thinking of how uncertain her future was now.

Rob was looking at her keenly. But fortunately, just then Luigi arrived to ask if everything was OK with their meal, stopping to discuss the football with Rob; and, much to her relief, the awkward moment had passed.

'I've been meaning to tell you,' Rob said over dessert. 'There's an old gentleman in the home who knew your grandparents — Bert Barnes.'

'Oh, I remember Mr Barnes!' Tamsin exclaimed. 'Grandpa Jim used to go to the football with him years back. At one time, he and his wife used to live next door to my grandparents and have a little draper's shop. The Barnes sold their property to my grandparents, who then extended the tea shop.'

'You know more about your family history than I do about mine,' Rob said in admiration. 'I suppose you wouldn't visit Mr Barnes? He's a lonely old gentleman now. He and his late wife were childless.'

Tamsin smiled. 'If you think he'd like to see me, then I certainly will. I'll mention it to Aunt Cathy. I'm sure she'd like to come too — although it mightn't be for a while, because things are a bit manic at present.'

'Well, I won't tell him he's likely to have any visitors for the moment, then.'

Rob had changed, Tamsin decided. He had developed a more caring attitude. She supposed he'd just matured. He'd probably make a very good nurse.

He slung an arm about her waist as they walked back to the car park. It was a balmy summer's evening and she'd enjoyed his company, but knew that was all. She'd changed too. They'd grown apart in many ways over the past years. She knew now, for certain, she didn't love him anymore. It was time for closure.

Presently, when Rob attempted to kiss her, she turned her head away so that his lips met her cheek. 'I'm sorry, Rob,' she told him. 'I'm delighted we've met up again, but time has marched on and we're both different people now. I'd like to think we can remain friends, but beyond that . . . There's no spark, Rob, and I'm sure you must have realised that.'

He took her hands between his. 'You're an incredibly nice person, Tam. I was wrong to have treated you so badly. We were teenage sweethearts and now we've moved on, but we'll keep in touch, eh? Meet up for the occasional drink for old times' sake?'

She nodded. 'I'd enjoy that, Rob, and I really hope all goes well for you.'

★   ★   ★

On Friday morning, Tamsin arrived at The Chocolate House to discover that, during the night, someone had adorned the side wall with an amazing display of graffiti.

'You've seen it, then?' Kelly asked, springing out from the doorway.

'Well, yes, I could hardly miss it. Someone's had fun with the spray can at our expense, haven't they?'

'Colourful, isn't it?' Kelly remarked.

'It certainly is — it'll be incredibly difficult to remove.'

Fraser's mobile was switched off, and Tamsin remembered him telling her he'd be at the factory most of the day. She left him a text message and hoped he would pick it up.

★　★　★

It was just turned three o'clock when a group of three teenagers came into The Chocolate House. It was obvious that Kelly knew them. They sat themselves at a table at the back of the café and, instead of going to the counter to give their orders, shouted across to her. She mixed milkshakes and dished out a plate of expensive cupcakes, but took no money.

Tamsin was in a quandary as to what to do. She decided to give them the benefit of the doubt. Perhaps they were going to pay the bill as they left. They lingered over their refreshments and, eventually, she had to go into the storeroom to fetch some more baguettes.

A loud shout and a scuffling sound sent her flying back into the café, just in time to see one of the teenagers disappearing outside, scattering several chocolates from the bowl on the counter in his wake.

To her amazement, Fraser had appeared as if from nowhere, and was shouting after him. Fraser then gathered up the chocolates and apologised profusely to the few startled customers in the café.

During the kerfuffle, the other youngsters had scarpered. Kelly seemed visibly shaken and Tamsin knew she was going to have to have a word with the girl about the incident. It was apparent that the teenagers hadn't paid their bill.

'Thanks, Fraser,' Tamsin said. 'If it hadn't been for your quick thinking . . .'

'I happened to be in the shop just now and was keeping an eye on them. It's obvious they didn't pay for their refreshments. No wonder the profits are down if this sort of thing happens on a regular basis. If I were you, I'd keep a tighter rein on what's going on,' he told her, grim-faced.

Tamsin's cheeks flamed crimson. 'Point taken, but unfortunately I can't be in two places at once, and Kelly needed some baguettes.'

'Strange — there's a pile on the shelf here,' he said in a matter-of-fact tone; and then, whistling, disappeared upstairs.

It was some time later when Tamsin managed to challenge Kelly about what had happened. 'You seemed to know that group of teenagers who were out to cause trouble, Kelly. I don't believe they handed over any money for their drinks and cakes.'

Kelly tossed her head and looked defensive. 'That was my brother and his mates. Vicki allows me to let my family and friends have free refreshments.'

'Actually, I understood the rule was half-price small drinks — definitely not freebies. And what about that young man who made off with those chocolates?'

'That wasn't my fault — I didn't know Ethan was going to do that. Please don't tell Vicki what happened. If I lose my job, I don't know what I'll do.' She sniffed and sat staring miserably into space.

Neither of them had noticed Fraser, who had come back downstairs just in time to catch most of the conversation.

'Do I take it you know those lads?' he asked Kelly, handing her a tissue from a box beneath the counter.

Kelly nodded. 'My brother and his

mates,' she repeated. 'Ever since Vicki threatened to cut my hours, Lee and the others said they were going to make trouble for The Chocolate House. I didn't ask them to, but my brother thinks he's looking out for me.'

'Well, he's got a funny way of showing it,' Tamsin said sternly. 'Which one's your brother?'

'The one with the spiky hair and the denim jacket.'

'Kelly, do you think they had anything to do with that remarkable display of graffiti and the break-in?' Fraser asked.

Kelly looked worried. 'Marvin did the graffiti, and they've had more freebies than they ought to have done a few times, but I'm sure they wouldn't do anything really bad.'

Tamsin got up to serve a couple of customers and saw Fraser was deep in conversation with Kelly.

'We're going to see Kelly's parents and talk things through with them, aren't we, Kelly?' he said when Tamsin joined them. 'Can you manage on your own until closing time, Tamsin? Kelly's not in any fit state to work at present, anyway.'

Tamsin agreed and Fraser went off with Kelly, returning alone about an hour later.

'So, have you managed to sort things out?' Tamsin wanted to know.

'Hopefully, yes. Both Kelly's dad and her brother were at home and we had a useful discussion. I don't think Lee and his mates will be causing us any more trouble. I'm sure they're not bad lads really — just high-spirited. Lee's going to be helping out around here in his free time until he's paid for all the freebies. We just need to get him fitted up with a work permit . . . '

He trailed off as he caught sight of the time. 'Sorry, I'll have to fill you in with all this later — ought to have been at the factory as of ten minutes ago. D'you fancy coming for a drive in the country this evening? We can chat over a quiet drink.'

'Go on, luv, sounds like an offer you can't refuse,' an elderly customer at the counter said, and winked at her. Colouring, Tamsin accepted the invitation, wishing it was a proper date.

Fraser sped up the stairs to reappear a few minutes later clutching a file. Pausing by the counter, he murmured in Tamsin's ear, 'I'll pick you up at seven-thirty,' before leaving the café.

* * *

It was a glorious summer's evening. They drove along narrow country lanes with fields on either side full of grazing sheep. At one spot there was a wooded area forming a green canopy overhead.

'Kent's full of surprises,' Fraser commented. 'It's so variable.'

Presently, they came upon a picturesque pub where people were sitting outside beneath colourful umbrellas, enjoying the last of the evening sunshine.

Over their drinks, Fraser filled

Tamsin in on what had happened. Apparently, Kelly's family were friendly with Marvin's; and fortunately, once the teenagers had owned up to what they had done, both sets of parents were extremely cooperative. Ethan's father worked for Clancy's and was horrified when Fraser told him what his son had been up to.

'So Marvin really was responsible for the graffiti?' Tamsin asked, reaching for her glass of wine.

Fraser grinned. 'Yes, he obviously fancies himself as another Banksy. His father's bringing him round tomorrow morning to make an attempt at cleaning it off. I wish them luck! It'll be a pain to remove.'

'So, what about the break-in?'

'Oh, all three have denied all knowledge of that, and I'm prepared to believe them. All the parents are keen to keep their sons out of trouble. Ethan's dad, Jeff, phoned me just before I left home tonight. He's dreaming up a suitable punishment to keep his young reprobate out of mischief. Lee's dad's approved my idea of getting his son to help in The Chocolate House.'

He paused to sip his beer. 'Who knows, if he proves his worth perhaps we can keep him on as a part-timer and pay him . . . What's wrong, Tamsin? You're looking dubious.'

'That's all very well, Fraser, but Bruce and Vicki have already told Kelly they'll probably have to cut her hours, *and* they had to let their Saturday lad go; so they're certainly not going to magic more money out of thin air to pay for Lee.'

Fraser reached out and caught her hands between his, making her pulse race. 'No problem. It was my idea, so it's my responsibility. I'll pay Lee's wages if they decide to employ him, and Kelly's additional hours too, so your cousins won't have to fork out anything extra.'

'You're all heart,' she said unsteadily, 'but what will you be gaining from it?'

He smiled at her. 'Oh, you'd be

surprised. Unfortunately, there are one or two things I can't divulge quite yet . . . Anyway, I'm hoping things will simmer down now,' he added optimistically.

'Let's hope you're right,' Tamsin told him. 'There's been enough drama for one day . . . What are you looking at?'

'I've just seen some mouth-watering desserts being served. How about sampling the strawberry tart and ice-cream?'

'But I've already had my supper at home,' she protested laughingly.

'So have I, but I can always make room for another pudding. Come on, let me twist your arm — the dessert will match your very becoming strawberry-coloured top. Oh, and I could do with some coffee, too.'

The dessert was sumptuous and, as they waded through it, they discussed their tastes in music, films and literature. The time sped by.

'I've thoroughly enjoyed this evening,' Fraser told Tamsin, as he pulled up outside her home. He leant over and, cupping her chin in his, kissed her gently on the mouth. A surge of emotion flooded through her and she wrapped her arms round his neck. The kiss became long, satisfying and beyond her wildest dreams.

After a while he released her. 'Sweet dreams,' he murmured against her hair.

* * *

At around ten o'clock the following morning, the door opened and a burly man entered with a subdued-looking teenager whom Tamsin recognised as one of the three miscreants from the previous afternoon. Fraser got up from the table, where he'd been looking through a sheaf of papers whilst he waited for them to arrive. After a few moments he beckoned Tamsin over.

'Marvin here's got something to say to you, Tamsin.'

Marvin shuffled his feet and looked embarrassed.

'Well, go on then, son, say your

piece,' his father prompted him. 'How on earth he thought he was helping Kelly by scribbling all over your walls and not paying for his eats and drinks beats me.'

Marvin went red and mumbled an apology.

'Look, let's all sit down over there and discuss things calmly over some coffee,' Tamsin suggested, aware that they were attracting the attention of some of the customers.

'Thought that's what caused the problem in the first place — free drinks,' Marvin's father grunted.

To Tamsin's amazement, once they were all settled with mugs of coffee Fraser said, 'So you fancy yourself as something of an artist, do you, young Marvin?'

The teenager nodded.

'Right then, when you've made an effort to clean that wall, supposing you come back another time and help me design some new flyers and posters for The Chocolate House? Obviously, I'll need to run the idea past Mr and Mrs Miles — who own this business — first.'

Marvin perked up and began to show an interest in what Fraser was saying.

'You can thank your lucky stars Mr Kershaw's prepared to be so lenient,' his father told him. 'You've fallen on your feet, son.'

Presently, when Fraser had gone outside with the other two to examine the wall, Kelly said, 'Fraser's all right, isn't he? Did he tell you I'm probably not having my hours cut, after all? I'm going to work really hard to make up for yesterday.'

Tamsin wondered how Rob could have thought Fraser wasn't a people person. He'd obviously done an excellent job in sorting things out with the teenagers. She smiled to herself as she remembered the previous evening and *that* kiss.

By lunchtime, Kelly and Tamsin were rushed off their feet. Unfortunately, Cathy was unable to help on this occasion as she was preparing for another dinner party.

Fraser collected up some empty mugs on his way to the counter. 'I've just been out to inspect the wall. Thought you'd like to know it's cleaner than it was before Marvin decided to decorate it, Tamsin. His dad obviously knew where to lay his hands on the right stuff.'

Tamsin looked up briefly from ladling soup into a bowl. 'That's good news. I'll take a look when I get a minute.'

'You look as if you could do with an extra pair of hands,' Fraser said. 'How about I help out for a while?'

Kelly, sorting out the coffee orders, looked at him in amazement.

'Don't look so surprised, Kelly. I've done a stint as a waiter before.' And, to prove it, he picked up the tray and marched off with it. Tamsin was grateful for his help as they were incredibly busy for the next hour.

Presently, during a lull, she sent Kelly

233

for her break. Shortly afterwards, the door opened yet again and Sue Morgan came in.

'Tamsin, you might just be able to save my life,' she announced dramatically.

'Why, whatever's wrong?' Tamsin asked in alarm.

Sue burst out laughing at her friend's expression. 'Sorry! Nothing serious. It's just that I'm desperate for some cake and the baker's is closed. Can I buy some of yours to take away? Danny's Aunt Bea is coming to tea and I've had no time to bake.'

'Well, we can't have Aunt Bea missing out on her tea!' Fraser said, setting down a tray of dirty crockery.

Sue laughed again. 'She's got a very sweet tooth. Whatever are you doing here, Fraser? Have you lost your job at Clancy's?'

'Hopefully not, although if I keep turning up late for meetings, my uncle might need to discipline me,' Fraser told her with a straight face. 'Now, I insist on buying you a coffee, and how about a slice of Cathy Lambourne's chocolate cake?'

'Well, I oughtn't to stop really, but how can I resist? Go on, then — just for ten minutes.'

Whilst Fraser was getting the coffee and cake, Tamsin fetched a box and Sue selected what she wanted to take away. 'I'm glad I've caught the pair of you — it's Danny's birthday next Saturday. We're having the usual family lunch next Sunday, but nothing on the actual day itself — so would you like to join us for a meal at our place?'

Tamsin saw the gleam in her eyes; and, knowing her friend of old, with her previous attempts at matchmaking, was convinced it had been a spur of the moment invitation.

'That would be delightful,' Fraser said, without a moment's hesitation. 'I'll make a note in my diary.'

'Good-o! How about you, Tam? Can you make it?'

Tamsin smiled. 'Yes, that would be

lovely, Sue,' she said genuinely, not meeting her friend's gaze.

Sue beamed. 'Great! I'll look forward to seeing you both at our place then — around eightish.'

Tamsin knew she'd look forward to the occasion too. She'd enjoy any time spent in Fraser's company.

10

On Sunday morning, Tamsin accompanied Aunt Cathy and Lucy to church. To her surprise, Fraser was there with his mother. After the service they all met up by the lych gate.

'What a wonderful day,' Georgina remarked. 'Hallo, young Lucy. What have you got there?'

'A sunflower,' Lucy explained proudly, holding the wobbly tissue-paper flower aloft for them to admire.

Cathy rested a hand on her granddaughter's shoulder. 'She's been to Children's Church, haven't you, dear?'

'Yes — hallo Fwaser — do you like my sunflower?'

'It's magnificent,' he said, stooping to the little girl's level.

Lucy rummaged in her pocket. 'This is a sunflower seed. I'm going to plant it on Gwandpa's 'lotment.'

'The theme was God's Creation,' Tamsin put in.

After a few more pleasantries, Cathy said briskly, 'Well, we'd better get on. We're taking the children on a picnic to the nature reserve.'

Lucy clapped her hands gleefully and Georgina Kershaw said somewhat wistfully, 'What a lovely idea. I'm not sure I've ever been there.'

'Well, why don't you join us?' Cathy invited impulsively. 'The more the merrier. We're a bit depleted today — what with Charlie being at Marissa's birthday lunch, and Vicki and Bruce being on holiday . . . Now, how about you, Fraser?'

Tamsin held her breath. Would he accept?

He ruffled Lucy's hair. 'Sounds fun. That'd be great. I very much enjoy picnics,' he told Cathy with a grin, and Tamsin felt a thrill of pleasure shoot through her at the prospect of spending more time in his company.

Georgina enquired about the food

and Cathy quickly assured her it was all in hand but, if she'd like to contribute some cold drinks, they'd be very welcome.

'We always get our teas and coffees at the cafeteria by the lake to save bringing flasks,' Cathy explained.

The picnic was a great success. They found a bench to sit at in a sheltered, wooded area. Georgina was very taken with the children, and Alec Lambourne was soon chatting to Fraser about his allotment. Tamsin wondered just how interested Fraser was in cultivating runner beans and marrows, but he surprised her by showing a fair amount of knowledge.

'My late uncle was a keen gardener and loved growing vegetables,' Georgina explained. 'Fraser spent a lot of time with him during his childhood and teenage years.'

'Well, we've got the Allotment Association Show Saturday week,' Alec informed them. 'So, if you're interested, please feel free to come along. There's an exhibition, and I can vouch for the refreshments because Cathy's lending a hand.'

'I really don't know how you manage to fit it all in,' Georgina said admiringly.

'Nor do I, sometimes,' Cathy smiled, wiping the egg from Jamie's face.

'Did Fraser mention he's got the decorators coming in to the flat next week? A couple of fellows Gerald Clancy uses who are keen to get some work.'

Cathy nodded. 'Yes, Tamsin's filled us in. I imagine the place could do with a facelift.'

'You know, I had no idea you used to live at The Chocolate House, Mrs Kershaw,' Tamsin remarked.

Georgina set down her scotch egg. 'Well, no, dear, it was many years ago; but you must have wondered how I came to know your grandfather and Cathy.'

'Well, yes, but when you returned to Stanfield I was working in the Midlands, so I suppose I missed out on all that, and then it didn't occur to me to ask.'

'It doesn't always do to ask too many questions in our line of business,' Cathy put in.

Fraser grinned. 'I expect you hear all sorts of things whilst you're serving the soup.'

'No, it's usually over the coffee and liqueurs when everyone's a bit mellow,' Tamsin quipped. 'We really have to guard our tongues sometimes.'

'Well, you might be interested to know that I used to work in your grandparents' tea shop,' Georgina volunteered. 'That's where I met Fraser's father.'

Tamsin's eyes widened. 'No, I'd no idea. I realised you'd lived in Stanfield previously, of course.'

Georgina had a faraway expression in her eyes. 'I came from the other side of Stanfield. My mother was a widow and rather hard-up, so I didn't stay on at school. I saw an advert for a waitress for the tea shop, applied, and got the job.

Your grandparents were so good to me.'

'So you must have known my father back then too,' Tamsin said slowly. She intercepted a look between her aunt and Georgina Kershaw and wondered why. Alec, who had been amusing the children, said brightly, 'I quite fancy a leg-stretch down to the lake. We can feed the ducks with the remains of our sandwiches.'

Tamsin was puzzled. Was there something they didn't want her to know about concerning her father? A family secret, perhaps? She was determined to find out.

The children fed the ducks with the leftovers and then everyone decided it was time for a cup of tea in the cafeteria. Tamsin and Fraser volunteered to fetch the drinks.

'It's strange to think your mother knew my father and Aunt Cathy all those years ago,' Tamsin remarked casually, as they sorted out the teas and coffees and added ice-cream cones for the children.

Fraser hesitated slightly. 'Well, I suppose it was inevitable she would have known your entire family if she worked in the tea shop. You know, sometimes, Tamsin, it's best to let sleeping dogs lie,' he advised and charged off with the tray, leaving her pondering over this cryptic comment. She was more convinced than ever that there was something her family was keen to keep from her.

Presently, she and Fraser set off for a short walk with young Lucy. Jamie was fast asleep in his buggy, and the others were happily discussing the economic situation.

'Let's go on a bug hunt,' suggested Fraser and, much to Tamsin's amusement, he produced a folding magnifying glass from his top pocket.

Lucy marched on ahead through the long grass to stop now and then and peer intently at a flower. 'Found one!' she shouted excitedly.

It turned out to be a ladybird, and after this, she spotted several butterflies, a couple of spiders and a lacewing. It was a pretty area with an abundance of wild flowers. Tamsin was able to identify mallows, toadflax and wild thyme.

At one point they turned briefly into a wooded area, and little Lucy ran back to them in alarm as a strangely eerie noise filled the air.

'Now that funny noise is a woodpecker,' Fraser told her. 'He's probably drilling a hole in the tree with his sharp beak.'

'However do you know all this?' Tamsin asked, fascinated.

'Oh, as my mother mentioned, I used to spend a lot of time in the holidays with her Uncle George. After his wife died, my maternal grandmother moved away from Stanfield to live with him and keep house. He had a cottage in the country — on the Kent and Sussex border. Anyway, what my great uncle didn't know about natural history, you could write on the back of a postage stamp; and his knowledge has obviously rubbed off on me.'

'It certainly has — I'm impressed . . . Lucy, come here, darling. Shall we go and look at the pond now?'

A group of children were pond-dipping, under the supervision of adults. It was a lovely spot and Tamsin could have stayed there all day. She and Fraser sat on a tree stump with Lucy between the pair of them. Fraser pointed out the brightly-coloured dragon- and damselflies, and the little girl watched entranced as they skimmed to and fro over the water.

'So what made your mother decide to return to Stanfield?' Tamsin asked curiously.

'Oh, memories. She has no family of her own left in Somerset now.'

She shot him a curious glance. 'I see. And what about you, Fraser?'

He was silent for a moment. 'Well, I obviously came here because of my mother, but that wasn't the only reason. As I've told you, the firm where I was working was relocating to London and, as I didn't want to go with them, I opted for redundancy.'

She had a feeling that wasn't the whole story.

Lucy wriggled on her perch. 'Look! A flutter-by!'

'Butterfly!' Tamsin chuckled. 'You are a funny girl. Shall we go and find the others now?'

'No! I want to stay here with you and Fwaser.'

'Well, that's nice,' Fraser said, 'but we might get hungry and want our tea.'

'Too tired to walk,' Lucy announced, and so Fraser obligingly gave the little girl a piggy-back. Tamsin liked this softer side of Fraser — so unlike the man she had encountered at Georgina's dinner party such a short time ago.

It had been a happy afternoon, and Tamsin was sorry it was coming to an end. She had so much enjoyed the time she'd spent with Fraser. With a sudden jolt, she realised she was falling in love with him.

On Monday morning the electrician was already at The Chocolate House by the time Tamsin arrived. Fraser had obviously let him in.

Tamsin frowned. 'I hope he doesn't need to turn off the electricity at the mains.'

'I doubt it, because there are separate meters in the flat; but if he does, then he'll have to come back after closing time,' Fraser assured her. 'Now, obviously I can't work from here today, but I'll drop by around lunchtime to see that everything's OK. Oh, and I should have mentioned — Marvin's father's coming round presently. It turns out he's a builder and has offered to help me sort out the back yard so that the workmen can use that entrance. It'll be easier for them to park in that vicinity, too.'

Tamsin served a couple of early customers. When she'd finished, she saw Fraser was still standing patiently beside the counter.

'There was something else, Tamsin. I thoroughly enjoyed yesterday afternoon and was wondering if you'd care to come out to dinner tomorrow evening?'

Tamsin's heart seemed to miss a beat. 'With you and Mrs Kershaw?'

He laughed. 'Not unless you feel the need for a chaperone! No, Tamsin, just with me.'

After she'd accepted, Tamsin realised she hadn't any idea where he was taking her and didn't have anything suitable to wear. When Aunt Cathy arrived with the freshly-baked cakes, Tamsin explained her predicament.

Cathy looked surprised. 'Fraser's taking you out! Well, then, you'll need to go on a shopping trip to find something smart to wear, dear. Look, I'll get your Uncle Alec to cover for a couple of hours tomorrow morning. Your hair could do with a trim too . . . Whatever's all that banging?'

Tamsin explained about the electrician. 'Fraser doesn't seem to be short of cash, does he?'

'Well, he's probably inherited something from his father's estate. The Kershaws are quite well off. Anyway, that's none of our concern,' Aunt Cathy said with her usual diplomacy. 'I suppose we should be grateful that Fraser's keeping the place in good repair.'

The following morning, Tamsin enjoyed her time out. She went to the hairdresser's for a trim, wash and blow-dry. She was pleased with her purchases: a floaty skirt in shades of sea-green; a scooped-necked white top with some neat embroidery, and a bolero that matched the skirt.

When she went downstairs ready to go out that evening her aunt raised her eyebrows slightly, and Charlie whistled.

'Very nice, dear,' Uncle Alec told her. 'You look charming.'

Fraser thought so, too, when he collected Tamsin at seven-thirty sharp. She looked so natural and unsophisticated. Her shining, fair hair tipped her shoulders and he could smell her floral fragrance. He acknowledged that this young woman was having an amazing impact on him. She was refreshingly different from the other girls he'd dated, including Petrina Hornby.

Fraser knew he was attracted to Tamsin in spite of his misgivings. When he'd left Bristol, he'd made a decision not to allow himself to get closely involved with any woman ever again.

Fraser had chosen a delightful restaurant hidden away in the Kent countryside, recommended to him by the Clancys. As they sat enjoying a glass of wine and studying the menu, Tamsin began to relax. The place was delightful and not nearly as ostentatious as she had feared.

Over their starters, Fraser told her about a concert he'd recently attended in the Barbican. She wondered who had accompanied him on that occasion. She supposed he had no shortage of female companions. She decided she'd just have to make the most of the time spent in his company, and intended to treasure every minute.

During a lull in the conversation she asked, 'So, are the electrics in the flat to your satisfaction?'

He smiled, reflecting that most women of his acquaintance wouldn't be the slightest bit interested. 'Yes, everything's absolutely fine, and the new power points will be very useful. Vicki and Bruce have assured me everything's fine with the shop and café areas. Health and safety are very rigorous these days. Stan's made a good start on re-decorating the sitting-room today, too.

'Later, when you've got a few minutes, I'd like you to take a look at some stuff in the boxes we've shifted to the spare bedroom. I think you might be interested.'

'What sort of stuff?' Tamsin asked, intrigued.

'Oh, mainly things about your family; a couple of books, photographs, letters — general memorabilia.'

'Goodness, perhaps Aunt Cathy or

Vicki should take a look first. They've probably forgotten about them.'

'Well, obviously I'll mention it to them, but I get the impression they're not so concerned with the past as you are, and so they might just want me to get rid of everything — whereas I think you'd find them of sentimental value.'

Tamsin found herself wondering just what he was referring to. She decided not to pursue it that evening.

Over their main course they talked about the various holidays they'd had, and generally got to know one another. She found herself comparing Fraser with Rob. Fraser showed a genuine interest in her, and she had to admit that Rob was more interested in his own pursuits.

The food was mouth-wateringly delicious, and Tamsin found herself thoroughly enjoying the evening and Fraser's company. They discovered they had a lot in common, including losing the fathers they'd both been so close to.

'So, have you still got family living in

Somerset?' she asked presently.

'Yes, a great-aunt and -uncle and their family on the Kershaw side. Their grandson is managing the Kershaw business — not my scene, I'm afraid, although I did work there for a few months some years back.'

'I see,' she said, suspecting there was quite a bit more he hadn't told her about his life in Somerset. 'So, what is the family business?'

Fraser looked surprised. 'It's a box-making factory. Amongst other things, it supplies Clancy's with the boxes for most of their chocolate products. Now, can you see how I might possibly be bored? Anyway, I've severed most of my ties now — sold the majority of my inherited shares.'

So that was how he was managing to pay for the improvements to The Chocolate House property!

'Anything else you'd care to know?' he asked, reaching for the dessert menu.

Tamsin went slightly red as she

realised she'd probably been a little too probing. 'No — no, I was just interested, that's all. When d'you think you'll be moving into the flat?'

He handed her the menu. 'As soon as the decorating's finished and the carpets are laid. I'll need to arrange for my stuff to be moved, although I haven't sold my property in Bristol yet . . . Now, have you decided what you'd like for pudding?'

Tamsin realised there were still things Fraser was not prepared to say about his past life, and wondered if he'd had a relationship that hadn't worked out.

Over dessert, their conversation turned to a safer topic as he asked her about the various places of interest to visit in the area.

'There are several castles and National Trust properties in Kent,' she enthused.

'Well, perhaps you'd like to show me some of them. My mother raves about Sissinghurst Castle, so that seems a good place to start.'

'I'd like that,' she breathed, eyes shining. 'It's one of my favourite places too.'

It had been a lovely evening. When Fraser pulled up outside her home, he reached across and gave her a searing kiss that satisfied her wildest dreams.

'Thank you, Tamsin, for a delightful evening. We must do it again soon.'

She went into the house feeling as though she were floating on air.

★　★　★

The following afternoon, Rob called in to see Tamsin at The Chocolate House. It was quiet so she was able to join him for a coffee. It was obvious he was bursting to tell her something.

'I've had a chat with the manager of the care home, and she thinks it would be an excellent idea for me to retrain as a nurse. Anyway, I've put it to my parents and they actually think it would be quite a positive step, so I'm going to make enquiries about submitting an application and whether any allowance would be made for my previous training . . . I can't believe all this has happened in the space of a week!'

'I'm so pleased for you, Rob, you've got a lot to offer,' Tamsin told him, 'but just promise me one thing.'

'What's that? If it's about the golf, then I've already decided it's definitely not for me! Think I'd be better sticking to table-tennis!'

'No, Rob, much as I love your sense of humour, sometimes it's necessary to take things a tad more seriously,' she said earnestly. 'If nursing is really what you want to do, then you must be prepared to give it your all.'

He nodded. 'Good advice, Tam. Thanks for being there for me. Alison was delighted when I told her, too.'

Tamsin raised her eyebrows. 'Alison? But I thought you weren't interested in Alison!'

He gave a wry smile. 'Well, you know how it is, Tam. I didn't want to hurt

your feelings, particularly as I'd promised to take you out for that meal.
There was no way I was going to treat
you badly twice; but then, when I
realised you really weren't interested in
me — apart from as a friend — I got to
thinking about Alison. Actually, I've
discovered we've got quite a bit in
common.'

'Well, just try to treat her properly,
Rob. I'm truly pleased things seem to
be working out for you.'

'You really are a very sweet person,
Tam,' he said softly. 'Thanks for
everything.' And grabbing her hand, he
pressed it to his lips.

It was unfortunate that Fraser came
into the café just in time to witness this.
Embarrassed, Tamsin pulled her hand
away.

'Hallo Fraser — come and join us for
a coffee.'

Fraser shook his head. 'Sorry, Rob,
I've a hundred and one things I should
be doing. Actually, I've just come to
check on the decorators so I'll push off

— sorry to have interrupted your *tête-à-tête*.' And he was gone before either of them could reply.

Rob rolled his eyes. 'Serious sort of guy, that one, isn't he?'

'Oh, Fraser's definitely got a sense of humour,' Tamsin assured him, 'but it's probably more subtle than yours.'

'So that's what I need to do, is it? Develop a more subtle sense of humour? Well, my old ladies and gentlemen appreciate my jokes — even if you don't.'

She was contrite. 'Rob, I didn't mean . . .'

To her relief he winked at her. 'No, you just meant — *remember, there's a serious side to life too.* OK, I'll work on my new, mature image. Now, tell me, Tam, how much longer are you going to be working in this place?'

'Well, Bruce and Vicki are due back on Sunday but not until late, so I expect I'll still be around on Monday — why?'

Rob surprised her by saying, 'You've

helped me make up my mind about my future career — now, what about you?'

Tamsin gazed thoughtfully into her coffee cup. What about her? It was true, wasn't it? She'd been busily sorting out other people's problems, but was no good when it came to sorting out her own.

'Oh, there's plenty to keep me occupied for the moment,' she said, but her stomach churned as she wondered for how much longer.

★   ★   ★

'Fraser's got a good idea for a promotion for The Chocolate House,' Tamsin told Aunt Cathy, as she set the table for supper that evening.

'Has he, now? Well, I'm not sure if Vicki and Bruce will appreciate too much interference. Anyway, whatever it is will have to wait until they get back . . . Leave the door ajar, dear, so that we can listen out for the children.'

The idea Fraser had run past Tamsin

had sounded great, and he wanted to get Marvin and Lee involved with handing out notices and flyers. But, of course, if Vicki and Bruce didn't approve, it would all come to nothing.

'Do you know what your uncle's suddenly reminded me about?' Cathy asked presently as she served up generous helpings of cottage pie.

Tamsin shook her head as she helped herself to peas and carrots.

'Apparently, I've promised to make cakes and sausage rolls for the Allotments' Open Day, Saturday week; to say nothing of taking a turn at serving the refreshments for an hour or so.'

'Right — well, I'll help out in any way that I can,' Tamsin assured her. 'It's not as if I'll be needed at The Chocolate House by then, is it?'

'Actually, I'm not so sure about that. Vicki will need a bit of catch-up time after her holiday, so you might be called upon to help out for a bit longer.'

'Don't you like working at The Chocolate House, Tam?' asked Alec.

'Yes, it's made a pleasant change, but there's a lot of office work piling up here,' she pointed out, and was surprised to intercept a glance exchanged between her aunt and uncle. She wondered what was going on.

'Well, dear, Lambourne Caterers is fast winding down. We've got bookings for another month or so, but I'm afraid that's about it,' Aunt Cathy told her.

Tamsin nodded. 'Yes, I've realised that, so I'm going to have to think long and hard about what I want to do next, aren't I? I mean, there's no way Vicki's going to be able to employ me in The Chocolate House, is there?'

'Oh, you never know what might be waiting for you round the corner,' Alec said optimistically. 'Now, what's for afters, Cathy? Am I right in thinking it might be treacle tart?'

11

Market day was always hectic at The Chocolate House. Aunt Cathy had been to lend a hand on Thursday morning. She then went off to fetch the children from nursery.

'Tamsin, is there any possibility you could take these two to the park for about an hour?' she asked on her return. 'That way, you can get some fresh air and I can stay here. Your uncle's busy working on his allotment. With the show just over a week away, he needs all the time he can get.'

'He'll miss it, won't he?' Tamsin said quietly and her aunt nodded.

Fraser appeared at the entrance to The Chocolate House just as Tamsin was struggling out with Jamie and the buggy. He gave her a hand down the step.

'We're going to feed the ducks,

Fwaser,' Lucy informed him, waving a bag of stale bread.

'Quack! Quack!' Jamie added, as if to reinforce the point.

'So I see. D'you think I could come with you? I like feeding the ducks too.'

'But weren't you just about to do something?' Tamsin asked, amused.

'Oh, I was only going to check on the decorators. They'll still be around when I get back, and your aunt's here to supervise young Lee if he shows up early.'

It was only a short walk to the small park, which was situated conveniently near to the library and information bureau. It was a glorious day and Tamsin breathed deeply. The sunlight filtered through the branches of the chestnut trees.

'Look, Fwaser, sqwirrel!' shouted Lucy, dancing up and down with excitement.

They wove their way along a series of paths to the duck pond, and spent several minutes feeding the mallards and watching one or two children with brightly-coloured toy boats. Afterwards, they went to the kiddies' playground, where Fraser obligingly pushed Lucy first on the swings and then on the roundabout, whilst Tamsin managed Jamie.

After a while, Tamsin strapped young Jamie back in the buggy and they began to walk back along the path. Lucy was happily running on ahead when a large, shaggy dog appeared from nowhere and bounded boisterously towards her, knocking the little girl over.

Lucy shrieked and, leaving Jamie to Fraser, Tamsin rushed over and scooped her up. 'You're all right, luv, just a little graze. I'll put a special plaster on it.'

Tamsin soothed the little girl and, rummaging in the bag on the buggy, found an antiseptic wipe and a *Mr Men* plaster.

'You're a natural at this,' Fraser said admiringly.

'Practice. Small children fall over. It's a fact of life.'

'Sweetie!' demanded Lucy.

'A reward for being a brave girl,' Tamsin explained to Fraser, scrabbling about in the bag again and coming up with a rather battered box of Smarties.

On the way back Fraser said, 'So, when does your cousin return?'

'Late on Sunday, so we're keeping the children until Monday.'

'So, no more trips to the park for you next week.'

'Oh, you never know. If I'm good, I might get allowed out,' Tamsin replied jokingly. 'Bruce and Vicki take it in turns to look after the children and the rest of us lend a hand when called upon. That's what families do, isn't it?'

Fraser smiled. 'Your rather haphazard working routine must play havoc with your social life. You and Rob must find it difficult to meet up.'

Tamsin stared at him. 'Until the night of your mother's dinner party, Rob and I hadn't seen each other for a considerable time. We . . . '

She trailed off as Lucy shouted, 'Fwaser, come and see what I've found!'

Fraser went to examine her find and the moment was gone. Now he would definitely think she and Rob were in a relationship, Tamsin thought miserably. She watched the little girl stooping to look at something, her hurt knee forgotten. Fraser knelt down on the grass beside her.

'It's a grasshopper,' he told her. 'Look, there it goes!'

There was a lump in Tamsin's throat as she watched them and recognised that, one day, Fraser was going to make someone a wonderful husband and be an excellent father to their children.

When they arrived back at The Chocolate House, Petrina Hornby was sitting at a table, nursing a latte and looking bored. 'Fraser, at last! Wherever have you been? Uncle Gerald's going to be away for a few days and needs to see you urgently before he goes. Your mobile was switched off, but your mother said you usually came in here during the afternoon.'

There was a silence and then Lucy said, 'Naughty Fwaser!'

Tamsin's mouth twitched. Fraser said, 'Well, I suppose I'd better get over there then.' He glanced down at his jeans which were covered in grass. She had never seen him looking so uncomfortable.

'Come into the back, Fraser, I've got a clothes brush,' Cathy offered.

'What on earth have you been doing — mowing the lawn?' asked Petrina, staring at his grass-stained trainers.

'We found a gwass-hopper,' Lucy said, helpfully.

'What? Oh . . . ' Petrina gave a little trill of laughter and finished her coffee.

Once they'd gone, Aunt Cathy said, 'I saw Fraser helping you with the pushchair earlier and guessed he'd gone with you to the park.'

'She wasn't well pleased, was she?'

Kelly remarked. 'Is that Fraser's girl-friend, then?'

'I really wouldn't know, dear,' Cathy said smoothly. 'They're work colleagues, but beyond that . . . Now, as Lee's wiping the tables, could you collect up those dirty mugs, please?'

★ ★ ★

That evening, as they sat over supper, Cathy made an announcement which stunned Charlie and Tamsin. 'Alec's put the house on the market today.'

Charlie's head shot up. 'Already! But, I thought you were going to wait for a few weeks!'

'Well, we've decided to get things moving. Apparently, there's quite a lot of demand in this area for this sort of family house,' his father explained.

'I see,' Tamsin said dully. 'OK, I suppose Charlie and I had better start looking around for alternative accommodation — in case there's a quick sale.'

'Oh, it's not likely to be that quick, dear,' Cathy assured her, 'but we thought we'd better mention it because it'll be in the paper and on the internet shortly. So we intend to let everyone know our plans for the future ASAP.'

'Sam's really desperate for some help, so I'm thinking of going to Norfolk for a few weeks just to get the feel of things,' Alec told them.

'Apparently, Sam's co-worker's keen to retire at the end of August. At least we've got the allotment show to look forward to. I'm so pleased I can get one last show in before I have to give up my allotment.'

'So is Bruce going to take it over when you move?' Charlie asked.

'No, I'm afraid it doesn't work like that — there's a waiting list. Anyway, Bruce is doing very well with his little veg patch, although he's enjoyed having some of our produce to supplement what he grows.'

'It seems impossible to think Vicki and Bruce's fortnight's up already,'

Cathy remarked. 'Are you OK to carry on working at The Chocolate House at least until Tuesday, Tam?'

Tamsin nodded and began clearing the table.

'I'm sure you must be champing at the bit to get back to the office and start sorting out the books. I'd no idea there'd be so much work entailed in winding up a business.'

Alec turned to his niece. 'Have you had a reply to the e-mail you sent to your mother, Tam?'

'Not yet, but it isn't always easy for them to reply straight away.'

Cathy got to her feet. 'Well, I'm sure Vanessa will ask you out to Africa when she learns of our plans.'

'But, even if I did go out there for a visit, the problem would still be here on my return, wouldn't it?' Tamsin pointed out as she stacked the dishes on the draining board.

Cathy took an apple pie from the oven. 'Well, you're quite versatile and you've got good qualifications, so there's bound to be an opening for you somewhere, dear.'

Tamsin met Charlie's sympathetic gaze. She sincerely hoped her aunt was right because she hadn't a clue as to what she was going to be doing beyond the next few weeks. Perhaps she ought to consider going to Africa, after all.

★   ★   ★

The surprise dinner for Danny's birthday was a great success. On their arrival, Fraser handed him a couple of bottles of wine from a local vineyard.

'I didn't know what we were eating, so I've brought both red and white.'

'Wonderful. Thanks — come on through. What are we eating, by the way, Sue?'

'Ah-ha, you'll have to wait and see.'

Tamsin handed Danny a gift-wrapped box of Clancy's chocolate-coated brazil nuts, which she happened to know he was partial to.

Sue was a perfectly competent cook,

but very laid-back, so Tamsin accompanied her friend into the kitchen to assist, knowing from past experience that otherwise they were likely to end up eating at ten o'clock.

'So, how's it going with you two?' Sue asked, opening the oven door and peering in at the chicken dish.

'Oh, we get on well enough,' Tamsin said carefully, determined not to give herself away.

Sue looked disappointed. 'He's gorgeous, Tam. I'd hoped you and he might . . . ' She trailed off as Danny came into the kitchen in search of a bottle-opener.

'Fraser's dug out another batch of postcards,' he told them, as he rummaged in the drawer. 'Mostly of Clancy's factory.'

The evening was a relaxed, enjoyable occasion with a great deal of laughter.

'It's a great pity the next meeting of The Postcard Society's had to be postponed,' Danny remarked presently, as they sat over coffee. 'Terry at the pub's suddenly discovered the room's double-booked.'

'Oh, well, we'll certainly have plenty to talk about next time round, and the group will be made up to see those postcards Fraser's unearthed,' Sue said. 'Several members work for Clancy's — including you, of course, Fraser.'

Fraser glanced at Tamsin. 'And I've just discovered a number of other postcards at The Chocolate House that I'm sure would be of interest to the group — that's if Tamsin's family don't mind loaning them out.'

'Oh, is that what you were telling me about the other day?' she asked, grey eyes full of interest.

'Yes, amongst other things. When you get the opportunity, perhaps you can take a look.'

Tamsin smiled at him, and for a moment, it was as if there were just the two of them in the room. Fraser thought how attractive she was looking that evening. She was wearing a simple, but stylish, print dress in shades of blue. Her shining fair hair seemed to have golden lights and he loved the way it flicked up at the ends. He could smell the sweet fragrance of her, and felt a deep pang of regret. If only she wasn't already involved with Rob, things might have been very different between them.

It was late when Fraser dropped Tamsin back home. He caught her hands between his. 'It's been a great evening, Tamsin. They're a delightful couple and it was good of them to invite me.'

He made no attempt to kiss her on this occasion and, as she entered the house, she suddenly felt desolate, knowing that she craved more than just friendship from him.

*   *   *

It was Tuesday morning when Vicki put in an appearance at The Chocolate House. She looked the picture of health and had acquired a tan.

'I've had a wonderful time in Spain

— lots of sun-bathing, swimming and good food. Thought I'd just pop in to find out how things are with you here . . . Now, Tam, do you think you can continue to hold the fort for a while longer? Bruce and I have got a meeting with Fraser Kershaw at Lavender Lodge later this morning.'

Kelly went pale and, noticing this, Vicki said, 'Yes, young lady, you've got some explaining to do. I'll speak with you later.'

After a few minutes during which Tamsin served several customers, Vicki said, 'You look as if you've been doing a grand job; we're sorry for any unnecessary aggro you've had. Anyway, Tam, I'll need to have a chat with you too, later on.'

Tamsin nodded. Obviously her cousin's holiday had done her good, and she was raring to get back to work. 'The decorators are still here,' she explained as there was a sudden thud overhead.

'Oh yes, of course. How are they getting on? Do you know?'

'OK, I think, although I haven't actually been up there since they've started work.'

* * *

Vicki returned from the meeting all smiles. 'Tell you later,' she said quietly to Tamsin. 'Come to supper tonight. We've got quite a bit we'd like to discuss with you.'

Tamsin supposed her cousin wanted to be brought up to date with what had been happening over the past fortnight.

Vicki signalled to Kelly, who followed her reluctantly into the kitchen. Tamsin didn't know what her cousin said to the younger girl, but she reappeared in the café presently, looking relieved.

'Vicki's giving me another chance,' Kelly said quietly. 'I know it's more than I deserve and I've promised I won't let her down again.'

'I should hope not,' Tamsin told her, pleased that her cousin had been so lenient.

It was late afternoon when Fraser put in an appearance. Tamsin hadn't seen him since Saturday evening. He went up to the flat and reappeared fifteen minutes later.

'They've made a splendid job up there. I'm arranging for the carpets to be fitted shortly. It's looking more like home every day. They assure me they'll be finished by Thursday, at the very latest.'

He waited until she'd finished serving a customer. 'I've had a chat with Vicki and Bruce this morning, Tamsin, and some of what we've discussed concerns you.'

'Me!' she exclaimed, startled. 'I'm not sure I like the sound of that!'

Fraser smiled. 'Oh, I can assure you there's nothing to worry about — quite the reverse, actually. I've been invited to supper with Bruce and Vicki tonight and gather you have too, so we'll talk then.'

Tamsin was more curious than ever and her mind worked overtime as she tried to guess what it was all about.

When Tamsin arrived at her cousin's house that evening, Bruce was upstairs putting the children to bed and Fraser hadn't yet arrived. Vicki ushered her into the sitting-room.

'So, what's all this about, Vicki? Fraser tells me you've invited him too. It all seems rather mysterious.'

'I'll come straight to the point, Tam. Mum tells me you've really fitted in well at The Chocolate House — have you enjoyed working there?'

'Absolutely. It's made a pleasant change.' Tamsin wondered where this conversation was leading.

Vicki picked up Jamie's teddy bear from the sofa. 'The thing is, Tam, I'd like to cut back on my hours. Mum tells me the catering work's beginning to dry up now — so Bruce and I were wondering how you'd feel about continuing at The Chocolate House for — let's say a couple of half-days a week to begin with.'

Tamsin stared at her cousin in surprise. 'Well, er — yes, why not? That'd be great, but you do realise I'm going to have to look for some more permanent work, because I'll need to earn enough money to rent a place of my own when your parents' house is sold.'

Vicki produced her trump card. 'Ah, now, we've come up with another idea about your predicament, Tam. I'm going to need quite a bit of help when the babies are born. Mum obviously didn't know I was pregnant when she told me she was moving, and now she's feeling guilty. I'm aware she and Dad are champing at the bit to get on with their new life in Norfolk, so I mustn't be selfish.'

She paused. 'She's promised to come and stay with me for a while when the twins are born, which will be great — but Bruce and I have been thinking, Tam. You're excellent with the children, so how would you feel about moving in here when the house is sold and helping out with Lucy and Jamie; and, of course, the babies?'

This was so completely unexpected that, for a moment, Tamsin remained silent. 'My goodness, Vicki, you've taken my breath away! I don't know what to say. You mean I'd be a sort of au pair?'

Vicki smiled. 'Well, a bit more than that . . . Look, you have a think about it and let us know. We do realise you might have your own plans for the future.'

'What I don't understand, Vicki, is where you're going to find the money to pay for all this with two more babies on the way,' Tamsin said bluntly.

'Ah, well, obviously Bruce and I have talked things through, and there is a way round it that will benefit us all. We'll explain things more clearly over supper because it involves Fraser.'

'Fraser!' Tamsin echoed.

As if on cue, the front door bell rang. 'That'll be him now. Can you let him in whilst I go and check on the meal?'

Tamsin nodded, feeling more mystified than ever.

★ ★ ★

The chilli con carne and rice was superb. During the meal, Fraser and Bruce had an in-depth discussion about the merits of growing one's own fruit and vegetables, whilst Vicki gave Tamsin a colourful account of their holiday in Spain.

It wasn't until they were finishing their dessert of cherry tart and ice-cream that Fraser said, 'That really was a most delightful meal, Vicki. Thanks so much. Now, do you want to fill Tamsin in with what we've been discussing, or shall I?'

Bruce and Vicki suggested it should be Fraser, and he rested his chin on his hands, surveyed her with his expressive dark-blue eyes, and said: 'It seems to us, Tamsin, that you've been left out of the loop in practically all that's been going on recently.'

'Yes, but that goes for Charlie as well,' Tamsin told him. 'We knew there was something the rest of you weren't telling us.'

'We had to wait for the right moment,' Bruce said. 'Cathy and Alec are filling in Charlie this evening, too.'

'Go on, I'm listening.' Tamsin looked at Fraser intently, unable to imagine what she was about to hear.

He smiled at her. 'I'm buying into The Chocolate House, which will take some of the financial worries and other pressures from your cousins' shoulders.'

Tamsin stared at him in stunned silence as she tried to get her head round this. Finally, she asked, 'But why? Why would you want to buy into a business that isn't exactly lucrative at the present moment?'

She saw Vicki was about to protest. 'No, come on, Vicki, Let's be realistic. I'm sure Fraser must have taken a look at your accounts.'

Fraser nodded. 'I certain have, and — in answer to your question, Tamsin

— I think The Chocolate House deserves another chance. I can see the potential, and believe that with a few good promotions and the right sort of marketing we could put it back on the map.'

Tamsin gave him a searching glance. 'So, let's get this straight. You're putting money into the business — in what way? Just to make it more upmarket with fancier décor, perhaps?'

Fraser leant back on his chair. He hadn't expected Tamsin to give him a hard time. 'Not to begin with, *no*, that's certainly not my intention. First we're going to sort out the security and reorganise things, so that it's not so easy for people to get in and out of the shop without us noticing.'

'Fraser's suggested he pays half of the wages and sorts out the promotions and security,' Bruce put in. 'Everything else will carry on as before for the time being. Obviously, we'll be sharing in the profits.'

Fraser nodded. 'I'll be taking a back seat at first and continuing with my own projects, but as time goes on, I hope to become more involved.'

'Well, I don't know what to say,' Tamsin told them. 'You're certainly full of surprises, Fraser.'

Shortly afterwards, Vicki and Bruce ushered the pair of them into the sitting-room. 'I'm sure there must be a lot the two of you want to discuss,' Bruce said firmly. 'I'm going to check on the children and help Vicki load the dishwasher, and then we'll have coffee.'

Left alone with Fraser, Tamsin suddenly felt vulnerable. The situation suddenly seemed too complicated for her to get her head round. If only Charlie were there.

'Come on, Tamsin, surely the news isn't all that bad, is it?' Fraser asked softly.

'It's all so sudden,' she murmured, '*and* I still don't think you've told me the whole story. We're in a recession, so why would you pour money into a struggling business when the world's your oyster?'

Fraser studied his hands. 'I have my reasons. Your grandparents were really good to my family years back, and I'd like to repay some of that kindness by helping out your family.'

She was puzzled. 'But why haven't I heard my grandparents mention you over all these years?'

Fraser paused, as if deciding what to tell her. 'Well, for a start, we lived quite a distance apart, remember . . . But, yes, there is something else I need to tell you that'll probably surprise you. I explained that I was born over The Old Tea Shop?'

Tamsin nodded, looking at him intently, as she wondered what other revelations he was going to make.

'Your father was my godfather, Tamsin.'

She stared at him in amazement. This was something she hadn't expected to hear. 'So why didn't I know?'

He hesitated. 'Oh, it's a bit compli-cated; but, as you've said, your father worked away a lot of the time. Anyway, my father brought me up to London whenever yours was in England, so that we could meet up for a day.'

'So your mother and mine didn't come on these outings?'

He shook his head. 'No, it was strictly the three of us. And then, after your father died, I continued to keep in touch with your grandparents, but sadly, I didn't get to see them; what with exams, and then university and a gap year, and — well, life in general.'

There was a pause and then Tamsin said, 'I get the impression that perhaps your mother didn't hit it off with my father.'

Fraser was silent. There had been enough revelations for one day and he knew that Tamsin would find the rest of the story difficult. 'It's water under the bridge,' he said at length.

'Is that why you appeared a bit hostile towards me when we first met?'

Fraser shook his head. 'Absolutely not. After all, I didn't know who you were at first, remember. No, the reason I was so impatient that evening was because I was concerned for my mother and wanted to be at her side — rather than at Lavender Lodge with people I barely knew. Throwing a dinner party seemed an inappropriate thing to be doing in the circumstances.'

'And all the mishaps caused by us made things even worse,' Tamsin added.

'Well, it certainly didn't help matters,' he agreed with a grin, and she had to smile too.

He flung an arm about her shoulders and drew her close; her heart pounded.

'Whatever happened between our families all those years ago needn't affect us, need it? It's time to move on.'

She agreed, even though she couldn't begin to imagine what he meant.

He pressed his lips against her hair and traced the line of her cheek, and then his lips found hers and he kissed her in a way that left her senses reeling. She wound her arms round his neck and kissed him back.

When Bruce and Vicki came into the room with a tray of coffee a few minutes later, Fraser was examining a toy of Jamie's and Tamsin was innocently flicking through one of Vicki's fashion magazines.

'Well, I've filled Tamsin in with the godson bit,' he said and, looking up, she saw him shake he head almost imperceptibly as if someone had asked a question.

Tamsin wondered what it was they were keeping back from her. She was determined to tackle Charlie when she got home, to see if he could throw any light on the matter.

However, it seemed Charlie knew even less than she did. He frowned. 'You say Fraser Kershaw is — was — your father's godson? Well, that's news to me — I'd absolutely no idea.'

'I feel sure there's something else, Charlie. Something no-one's prepared to tell me,' she said worriedly.

'A skeleton in the family cupboard? How fascinating! Well, I'm sure it can't be that ominous. If I find anything out you'll be the first to know.'

Tamsin had to smile. 'Thanks, Charlie, but I get the distinct impression the others know already!'

12

For the rest of the week, Tamsin saw virtually nothing of Fraser. She spent a lot of time in the office attempting to catch up on the book-keeping. Now that the catering business was in the process of being wound up, there seemed to be an enormous quantity of paperwork to deal with.

Uncle Alec was spending every available moment at the allotment, and Aunt Cathy seemed extremely preoccupied, as usual, with a variety of different tasks, including a huge bake for the open day that Saturday.

Fortunately, Saturday dawned bright and sunny for the Allotment Association's open day. It was early afternoon when the public had been invited to look round.

Uncle Alec was almost bursting with pride, as he told his niece he'd been awarded several prizes in the marquee. There were, he added, one or two other surprises.

When Tamsin entered the marquee, she discovered Uncle Alec had won first prize for his runner beans, carrots and marrow, and second for his soft fruit.

'Well, your family have been busy! They've swept up numerous prizes. I'm impressed!'

Looking up, Tamsin saw Fraser smiling at her and her heart missed a beat.

'Oh, has Aunt Cathy won something too?' she asked, acutely conscious of his closeness.

For an answer, Fraser took her arm and steered her towards the home-baking sections where Cathy had taken a prize for both her raspberry tart *and* her rhubarb-and-ginger jam. He then guided her towards the children's section where Lucy had won a prize for her pressed-flower picture.

'Oh, she'll be delighted. She put so much effort into it, bless her! She painted her fingers and pressed them onto the paper for the stems — with a little guidance, of course. And she spent ages pressing those flowers and sticking them on.'

'Well, that's not all — there's the piece de résistance.'

'Whatever are you talking about, Fraser? There can't be anything else.'

This time he took her arm and led her to the other side of the marquee where there was an adult craft section. She gasped as she saw the rosette for first prize; awarded to her for her decoupage picture of Uncle Alec's allotment that she'd made for his birthday earlier that year.

'I'd no idea he'd entered it!'

Fraser slipped a casual arm about her shoulder. 'You and your family are very talented, Tamsin, and today proves it.'

Just then Georgina Kershaw came up to them. 'My dear, many congratulations for that wonderful picture. Whatever are we going to do next year without your family's contributions?

I'm absolutely devastated by your aunt's news about moving to Norfolk. My dinner parties will never be the same without Lambourne Caterers!'

Fraser was completely taken aback. 'What's this? I've only just got to know your family, and now you're going away!'

'I honestly haven't a clue how we'll manage when it comes to entertaining,' Georgina said.

'Fraser will have to lend a hand,' Tamsin told her lightly, meeting his gaze steadily.

Fraser pulled himself together with an effort. 'You may mock, but I can produce a perfectly good roast dinner. It's just a pity you're not going to be around long enough to sample it.'

With a jolt, Tamsin suddenly realised they thought she and Charlie were uprooting too. Before she had a chance to put matters right, a friend of Georgina's tapped her on the shoulder.

'Come and look at my flower arrangement. I've won second prize!'

And, after a moment, the trio moved off, leaving Tamsin feeling miserable at the way things had been left.

* * *

The following week, Tamsin did a couple of stints at The Chocolate House. Every time the door opened in the late afternoon, she held her breath wondering if it might be Fraser, until it suddenly dawned on her that he was most probably using the back entrance.

On Friday, Georgina came into The Chocolate House. 'I've been speaking to Pauline Wise in the post office,' she told Tamsin, when she fetched her order. 'I'm afraid I'd got my wires crossed. I'd understood you and Charlie would be moving to Norfolk with Cathy and Alec. It wasn't until Pauline told me that Charlie would be moving in with her, Don and Marissa when the house was sold, that I realised my mistake.'

Tamsin swallowed and tried hard to

act normally, even though Charlie's news had come as a surprise to her. 'Yes, well, he gets on very well with the Wises.'

Georgina reached for the sugar. 'So, what about you, Tamsin? Where are you going to live? To say nothing of your job.'

'Oh, that's all been taken care of,' Tamsin said airily. 'In the short term, I'll probably be moving in with Vicki and her family. I'll be doing a few shifts here, like I am now, and helping out with the children to give Vicki a bit more free time.'

'Really? Well, that's nice, dear. Am I right in thinking there's going to be an addition to Vicki's family?'

Tamsin's eyes widened. 'Well, actually, yes, although it isn't common knowledge yet — how did you know?'

'Oh, your Uncle Alec hinted as much but, in any case, I guessed. She's suddenly looking so bonny.'

As she was leaving Georgina said, 'Fraser's gone to Bristol for the

295

weekend to sort out his house. Petrina Hornby's gone along with him.'

Tamsin murmured something politely and turned away to serve a customer, a dull ache in her throat. She supposed Petrina was far more his type — attractive, well-dressed and lively company. Not for the first time, she felt a pang of envy.

On the following Tuesday afternoon, Fraser arrived at the café just as Tamsin was about to close up. 'When would be a good time to look at that stuff I've unearthed belonging to your family?' he asked.

Tamsin had thought he'd forgotten. 'Now?' she suggested. 'I'm not in any particular hurry.'

She followed him up the stairs. The newly decorated sitting-room looked bright and airy. The walls were cream and the carpets a delicate shade of green.

'So, what d'you think?' he asked, watching for her reaction.

'It's lovely, but it'll look even better

when you've got some furniture and curtains.'

He laughed. 'Yes. I've decided to rent out my house in Bristol for a while. The furniture isn't right for here, but I've brought a few bits and pieces back with me, and my mother's letting me have one or two items of hers that are surplus to requirements. The rest, I'll have to get gradually. I intend to scour the antique shops, but for the time being, we'll have to make do with these.'

He indicated a couple of folding garden chairs. When they were seated he gave her a keen look. 'Why did you let me think you were going to Norfolk with your aunt and uncle, Tamsin?'

'It was a misunderstanding,' she told him, cheeks flaming.

'There seem to have been rather a number of those,' he said quietly. 'I had an interesting conversation with my cousin Robert the other day. I quite thought you two were in a relationship, but he assures me you're just good friends nowadays.'

'Why would it matter to you?' she asked unsteadily, her heart beating rapidly.

He didn't reply but got to his feet abruptly. 'I'll go and fetch that stuff,' he told her and left the room, to return a few minutes later with a box which he deposited on the carpet in front of her. 'Have a look through those whilst I make us some tea.'

When he brought in the tea-tray, she was studying some postcards that her father had written to her grandparents. 'I didn't realise all this existed,' she said, wondering why Aunt Cathy hadn't shown them to her before. There were several letters too. At the bottom of the box were a couple of books, a number of loose photographs and a bundle of postcards of Stanfield.

'Have you looked at this stuff, Fraser?'

'Not really, apart from the postcards. I naturally glanced at some of it, but when I realised it was rather personal, I didn't delve any further. I take it they're things that would interest you?'

'Absolutely,' she said, her eyes shining. She held up the book of *Hans Anderson's Fairy Tales*. 'I can remember Dad reading me stories from this book when I little.'

Whilst Fraser poured the tea, Tamsin thumbed through the photographs. There were a number of group pictures taken outside The Old Tea Shop, and several others of her father with a pretty blonde-haired woman whom she didn't recognise.

She frowned. 'I've absolutely no idea who this woman is — have you, Fraser?'

Fraser set her tea on a crate he was using for a table and took the photographs from her. There was a curious expression on his face as he glanced at them. 'Yes,' he said slowly. 'That's Aunt Ellen — my godmother. She was my mother's best friend.'

'The one who died recently?' Tamsin prompted, even more mystified.

'That's right.' He took a sip of tea, as

if to fortify himself. 'I'm surprised your family haven't said anything to you over all these years.'

'My family are very good at keeping things to themselves. So, come on, then — you'd better tell me what it is you think I ought to know.'

Fraser hesitated and then said in a rush, 'When I was born, your father and Ellen were engaged. That's why they were chosen to be my godparents.'

Tamsin stared at him in amazement. 'My father and your mother's friend, Ellen. I'd no idea. So what happened?'

'Your father met your mother just weeks before the wedding. She came into The Old Tea Shop one day, and they fell head over heels in love.'

'So, Dad called off the wedding and married my mother instead. Wow!'

They sat in silence for a few moments, each immersed in their own thoughts. Tamsin thought it was one of the most romantic stories she'd ever heard. She found it difficult to believe that no-one had told her about it before.

Fraser replaced the photographs in the box. 'As you can imagine, Aunt Ellen was devastated. Your father had been her entire world, but it would have been very wrong of him to have married her when he loved Vanessa.'

'So, I suppose it created bad feeling between your mother and my father?'

He nodded. 'I'm afraid so. You see, my mother felt responsible having introduced Aunt Ellen to your father. She couldn't forgive him.'

'So, was that when you moved away from here?' she asked, fascinated.

'Not immediately, no. It was your father who moved. Your grandparents were very unhappy with the situation. They'd been fond of Aunt Ellen. Your father went to stay with a friend and married your mother a few months later. As you're aware, they travelled around quite a bit, and only returned to Stanfield when you were about three or four.

'By that time, my own parents had

decided to move to Somerset so that my father could work in the Kershaw family business.'

'Oh, so that's how you came to be living in Somerset?'

'Yes, that's another story. My father fell out with his stepfather, Mathew Clancy, when he announced he intended to marry my mother. Mathew didn't think my mother was good enough for his stepson, and threw him out of Lavender Lodge.'

'So that's how your parents came to be living here, in this flat, when you were born,' she breathed.

He smiled and placed an arm about her shoulders. 'Yes, the course of true love never runs smoothly . . . So, now you know why it was just the three of us that met up in London from time to time — your father, mine and myself. Perhaps my mother was behaving rather irrationally, but that's the way it was.'

'So, what made her decide to return to Stanfield after all those years away?' Tamsin asked curiously.

'Oh, she'd always had a hankering to return here. We'd been back on a number of occasions to visit our family and friends, and we'd always made a point of calling on your grandparents. In time, my mother came to realise that she'd been wrong to blame your father for what happened; but, by then, it was too late to put things right.'

He gave her a hug. 'Your father was a delightful man, and he didn't intentionally set out to hurt Aunt Ellen. We can't choose who we fall in love with, Tamsin.'

How true that was! There was a lump in Tamsin's throat, and she turned away, afraid that he might see the glimmer of tears in her eyes.

'After my father died, my mother suddenly realised that Stanfield was where she wanted to spend the remainder of her life. Sometimes really good things can come out of bad situations.

'My mother is blissfully happy at Lavender Lodge, and I hadn't a clue what the future held for me until she suggested I might like to come here too. At first, I wasn't at all sure if I wanted to own this property; but then, after I'd been here for only a short time, it felt as if I'd come home — and now . . . '

'And now you've met Petrina Hornby,' she said quietly.

He looked at her, astonishment in his blue eyes. 'Petrina? Well, yes, I've certainly met her. She's a very nice girl, but . . . '

He frowned. 'Tamsin, surely you don't imagine there's anything going on between Petrina and myself?'

Tamsin swallowed. 'She accompanied you to Bristol last weekend . . . '

'Well, yes. I gave her a lift because she hates driving long distances and her folk live in that area.'

'I see,' Tamsin said; and, feeling foolish, she scrambled to her feet.

Fraser got to his feet too. He caught her hands between his. 'Tamsin, there are things I need to tell you about myself. You see, when I . . . '

His mobile played a lively little tune; muttering beneath his breath, he snatched it up, had a brief conversation, and switched it off.

'Tamsin, I'm so sorry. People do choose their moments! I'm afraid I'm needed at the factory as of now ... But, before I go, I'd like to ask you something. If you're not partnering Rob, would you be my plus-one at Clancy's annual dinner dance next Saturday?'

It took a moment for his words to sink in. 'Really? But what about Petrina — won't she expect ...'

He laughed. 'No, she won't. Warren has introduced her to a friend of his who's much more her age. You've a very caring nature, Tamsin. Now, I'd best be off.'

He caught her gently by the shoulders and propelled her from the room; and then, locking the door securely behind them, dropped a kiss on her startled mouth before scuttling down the stairs.

Tamsin felt ecstatic. She'd never been to Clancy's annual dinner dance before, even though Vicki and Bruce had. To be partnered by Fraser was beyond her wildest dreams.

* * *

When Aunt Cathy learnt of the invitation she immediately told Tamsin to buy herself a new dress. 'After all, dear, we were happy to pay for your ticket to Africa, so it's the least we can do. Would you like me to come with you?'

Tamsin tactfully declined her aunt's offer. She'd seen the very dress she would like in the window of a smart little boutique in Stanfield. Fortunately, it was still there the next day. It was in beautiful muted shades of sea-green, figured with silver. The neckline was far more daring than she would normally have worn, but she was wearing it for Fraser.

The sales assistant assured her it

fitted beautifully. She bought a pair of sling-back silvery shoes and arranged to have her hair done at the hairdresser's Vicki frequented. She smuggled her dress up to her room, determined that no-one should see it before the evening of the dance.

Vicki lent her a wrap. 'Now, how about I do your make-up for you?'

With a smile, Tamsin shook her head. 'Thanks, but I'll manage to do my own. What's good enough for the Duchess of Cambridge is good enough for me!'

Fraser arranged a time to collect Tamsin, and she spent a long while getting ready. At last she came downstairs.

'You look incredible, Tam,' Charlie told her, and Aunt Cathy and Uncle Alec agreed.

When Fraser knocked on the door a short while later he stood and stared at her. 'You've rendered me speechless,' he said at last. 'You look absolutely stunning. I've always wondered what you would look like if you really dressed up.'

She smiled, her heart singing. 'And you look amazing too.'

'Enjoy yourselves,' Aunt Cathy told them.

★   ★   ★

Clancy's annual dinner dance was held at a rather grand hotel on the outskirts of Stanfield that had formerly been a country mansion. Tamsin felt a little nervous, but Fraser took her arm and she immediately became relaxed. She knew quite a few people there, including the Averys.

Susan Avery looked frankly astonished when she caught sight of her. Her finely-pencilled eyebrows nearly shot into her hairline. 'Tamsin, I hadn't realised you were coming. Are you with your cousin?'

'No, she's with me, Aunt Susan,' Fraser told her. 'Doesn't she look gorgeous?'

Susan Avery, who was wearing an expensive-looking black number, said,

'Yes, very nice. So didn't Georgina want to come?'

'No, it's not really her scene,' Fraser replied and whisked Tamsin away.

Tamsin swallowed as something suddenly dawned on her. 'Fraser, have I taken your mother's place?'

'Absolutely not. If she had wanted to come, Uncle Gerald would have arranged it. After all, she is his sister-in-law. Don't take any notice of Aunt Susan, Tamsin.'

He took her across to Vicki and Bruce, who squeezed his wife's arm and said, 'Doesn't Tamsin look a million dollars?'

Vicki nodded. 'That's a beautiful gown, and Lucas has done wonders with your hair.' Coming from Vicki, that was praise indeed!

As they were going into dinner they passed Rob Avery, who said, 'Wow, Tamsin, I hardly recognised you. You look wonderful!'

For once, Tamsin *felt* wonderful. To her relief, they were sitting with Vicki and Bruce. The four-course meal was excellent, and she began to enjoy herself.

She glanced down the table. There were a number of people there that she knew from the dinner parties she had helped out at. Rob, catching her gaze, lifted his glass and smiled. He had brought Alison, who was wearing an astonishing dress in lime-green and black. It was strapless and low-cut, and Tamsin couldn't help wondering how she managed to get it to stay up.

The meal took a long time; and then, after coffee and more wine for those who wanted it, they got to the speeches. Tamsin must have switched off because she suddenly heard Fraser's name and realised he was getting to his feet.

Gerald Clancy waved a hand in his direction. 'My nephew, Fraser Kershaw, ladies and gentlemen, has already earned his keep by coming up with several innovative and original ideas for marketing our products. He's living above The Chocolate House, run by

Victoria and Bruce Miles who are sitting opposite him. That too is a good advert for our products — so if you're in Stanfield, why don't you pay it a visit sometime?'

Fraser sat down and Tamsin saw that his cheeks were faintly pink. 'I'm relieved that's over,' he murmured.

Shortly afterwards they moved into the ballroom. Fraser caught her arm and led her onto the dance floor. She loved dancing and felt totally exhilarated in his arms. Presently, they sat down and watched the whirling kaleidoscope of colourful dresses for a while. Tamsin felt happier than she could ever remember being before.

'Fraser, you never did finish telling me what you started to when your uncle phoned you the other week.'

'No, and I certainly intend to, but not tonight. If you're free tomorrow afternoon, would you show me the delights of Sissinghurst Castle? And then I'll finish the story.'

'I'd love to,' she breathed, eyes shining.

The rest of the evening passed in an enchanted manner. Tamsin had several dances with other partners, including Rob.

'Are you and Fraser . . . together?' he wanted to know.

'Well, I'm his partner for the evening,' she told him, eyes sparkling.

'Amazing! I never would have believed it!' he said.

Tamsin could hardly believe it herself. Presently, Fraser caught her by the arm and led her into the garden. It was a warm evening and several couples were strolling about.

'Ever since I met you, I've wondered what you would look like when you're really dressed up, and now I know. You look absolutely stunning,' he said and, slipping an arm about her waist, he guided her into a secluded part of the garden and kissed her in a way that left her senses reeling.

She wound her arms about his neck

and kissed him back. She knew that her memories of that evening would last for ever.

★ ★ ★

The garden at Sissinghurst Castle, created by Sir Harold Nicolson and his wife, Vita Sackville-West, was said to be one of the most famous in the world. Tamsin thought it was also one of the most romantic gardens she had ever visited. She had been there in all seasons, but loved the summer best.

Fraser put an arm about her waist as they strolled round it on Sunday, stopping now and again to exclaim over a spectacular flower display or to sniff one of the fragrant blooms. They took a look at the cottage garden, and lingered for a time in the white garden, which Tamsin thought was her favourite. It was full of roses, hibiscus, and clematis.

'I never tire of coming here,' she told him. 'Apparently Queen Elizabeth I stayed here in 1573, but all that's left of the original castle now is the tower.'

Part of it was open to the public, and after taking a look, Fraser suggested they had tea.

'So, are you going to tell me the rest of the story now?' she asked again.

He looked around the crowded tea-room and laughed. 'You're going to have to wait just a little bit longer, because I don't want to share what I've got to say to you with all these people.'

Presently, as they sat in the rose garden, he took her hands. 'At last I've got you to myself, so I can finish what I set out to say the other day.

'Tamsin, when I came to Stanfield a relatively short while ago, I was feeling a bit lost. You see, several months back, the woman I'd thought I was in love with had left me for someone else.

'I know now it would never have worked out between us. My pride was hurt, and I was determined to retain my bachelor status for the rest of my life . . . but then I met you, Tamsin Lacey, and things changed. Our families were intertwined years back. And now that's happening all over again . . . Tamsin, I've fallen in love with you.'

Her eyes shone as she told him, 'Oh, Fraser, I love you too.'

Suddenly she was in his arms; and he was kissing her as if he never meant to stop, and it was as if she had been waiting for this moment all her life.

THE END

We do hope that you have enjoyed reading this large print book.

Did you know that all of our titles are available for purchase?

We publish a wide range of high quality large print books including:
Romances, Mysteries, Classics
General Fiction
Non Fiction and Westerns

Special interest titles available in large print are:
The Little Oxford Dictionary
Music Book, Song Book
Hymn Book, Service Book

Also available from us courtesy of Oxford University Press:
Young Readers' Dictionary
(large print edition)
Young Readers' Thesaurus
(large print edition)

For further information or a free brochure, please contact us at:
Ulverscroft Large Print Books Ltd.,
The Green, Bradgate Road, Anstey,
Leicester, LE7 7FU, England.
Tel: (00 44) **0116 236 4325**
Fax: (00 44) **0116 234 0205**

Other titles in the
Linford Romance Library:

I'M WATCHING YOU

Susan Udy

Lauren Bradley lives a quiet life in her village flat, with only her cat for company. So why would anyone choose her as a target for stalking? As the harassment becomes increasingly disturbing, several possible candidates emerge. Could it be Lauren's old friend, Greg, who now wants more than just friendship? Sam, the shy man who works in the butcher's shop across the street and seems to know her daily routine? Or even handsome but ruthless Nicholas Jordan, her new boss to whom she is dangerously, but hopelessly, attracted?

FAIRLIGHTS

Jan Jones

The fortified pele tower of Fairlights, its beacon shining out across the harbour, has guarded Whitcliff for centuries. Sorcha Ravell thought she'd recruited the perfect restoration expert in Nick Marten — but he turns out to be dangerously attractive; knows more about her than she can account for; and is very, very angry. As the autumn storms build and the tension rises, Sorcha must overcome a paralysing physical fear and confront a terrifying mental enigma. What happened to her so many years ago? And why can she not remember?

DIFFICULT DECISIONS

Charlotte McFall

Tracy Stewart left the Derbyshire village of Eyam to pursue her dream of becoming a solicitor. Returning home for Christmas is the last thing she wants to do. A brush with Mike O'Neill starts to change her mind, but is it enough to make her stay? Mike has taken over running his father's bookshop, whilst working as a writer in secret. But can he keep his secret as well as the girl he loves?

TANGLED WEB

Pat Posner

After his beloved great-uncle has an angina attack, Jarrett tells his fiancée, Emily, that the elderly man's one wish is to live long enough to see him happily married. Emily agrees to bring their wedding forward but she's devastated when, on their honeymoon, she hears of a clause in Jarrett's great-uncle's will: the first baby boy born in the family will inherit the family business. Has Jarrett only married her so he can produce an heir before either of his brothers beat him to it?

SEE YOU IN MY DREAMS

Suzanne Ross Jones

When Vicky Simpson arrives from Edinburgh as a worried relative in nurse Ryan McGregor's hospital, there's an immediate attraction between the two. As a trained nurse herself, Vicky stays to help care for her brother-in-law. It proves impossible for Vicky and Ryan to avoid each other, and their attraction. But Vicky doesn't intend to stay in Aberbrig, and Ryan is firmly settled there. Should they nurture their growing romance? Or should they end things before someone gets hurt?

LIGHT THE CANDLES

Denise Robins

Who is the attractive stranger who knocks on the Cornells' door one snowy Christmas Eve? Lucy discovers the answers to a tragic family secret — and finds lifelong romance . . . Charlotte and Bill are happily married — until they have children, forcing Charlotte to choose between being a loving wife or a caring mother . . . Nicholas Carden is impossibly handsome — and a woman-hater. But Victoria is determined to marry him, by hook or by crook! Twelve tales of the heart by veteran author Denise Robins.